FINDING A *Happy* MEDIUM

LET THE REDEEMED SAY SO

THE SEQUEL

JANETTE JONES

Copyright © 2025 Janette Jones.

All rights reserved. No part of this book may be reproduced, stored, or transmitted by any means—whether auditory, graphic, mechanical, or electronic—without written permission of both publisher and author, except in the case of brief excerpts used in critical articles and reviews. Unauthorized reproduction of any part of this work is illegal and is punishable by law.

This book is a work of fiction, albeit, biblical personalities were utilized in the context of this fictional literary project. It is not the author's intention to rewrite or to minimize the factual aspects of the Holy Scripture. This work of fiction serves only as the author's contrived imagination of a world of 'what-if.'

ISBN: 979-8-89419-752-4 (sc)
ISBN: 979-8-89419-753-1 (hc)
ISBN: 979-8-89419-754-8 (e)

Because of the dynamic nature of the Internet, any web addresses or links contained in this book may have changed since publication and may no longer be valid. The views expressed in this work are solely those of the author and do not necessarily reflect the views of the publisher, and the publisher hereby disclaims any responsibility for them.

One Galleria Blvd., Suite 1900, Metairie, LA 70001
(504) 702-6708

Dedicated to Jaylen; my one and only grandson, and precious grand girls, Kenzle and Samaria.

See to it that no one comes short of the grace of God that no root of bitterness springing up causes trouble, and by it many be defiled.

—Hebrews 12:15

PROLOGUE

What happens when we die? Have you ever thought about it? It's an age old question many have pondered. The fact of the matter is no one truly knows…but God!

Yet, many would beg to differ as clairvoyant individuals known as 'mediums' or 'psychics' are readily enabling the living access to their supposedly loved ones from beyond the grave.

That's not to say, the practicality of it all must surely lie in their belief of the legitimacy of the practice. The question one must ask then is; is the practice of consulting the dead taboo, or is it God-designed?

With that in mind, it may interest one to know that God has already spoken on the matter as can be found in His Word.

> *"Do not turn to mediums or seek out spiritists, for you will be defiled by them. I am the LORD your God."*
> *Leviticus 19:31 NIV*

We also find in 1 Samuel 28:7 Saul the king of Israel going against his own decree when he at the time sought to inquire of such a being.

> *[7]Then Saul said to his servants, "Find me a woman who is a medium that I may go to her and inquire of her." And his servants said to him, "In fact, there is a woman who is a medium at En Dor."*

Ironically, Saul at one time sought to uphold Leviticus 19. It was only after Saul's rebellion of God's word did the Lord become silent. The king soon found himself in dire straits of needing to hear a word from God and soon took drastic measures. *"Find me a woman who is a medium..."* he commanded in 1 Samuel 28:7.

Where then does the sin lie? Possibly in the fact Saul sought to know the outcome of a war he would be involved in from a person under the influence of a 'familiar spirit,' a demon. Who knows, the king's fate could've been much different had he trusted in the Lord for a victorious outcome. Only God is omniscient (knows all and sees all). He knows the end from the beginning.

The written Word of God in today's society is often thought of as obsolete. Some will go so far as to declare "there is no God" and tend to seek knowledge meant only to be known by God through artificial means.

Take for example, just for the sake of 'what if; what if a spiritual portal would develop allowing the likes of Hebrew 12's 'cloud of witnesses' access to the 'here and now?' Then would the nay-sayers (atheists/agnostics) recant their un-belief?

Or, what if their divine messages could give first-hand knowledge of just how real our God truly is?

Better still, what if Biblical personalities with questionable character; such as 'the witch of En Dor,' or even the 'Woman caught in adultery' could tell their own version of their sordid lives?

Well... hold on to your seats! Just as the critically acclaimed parody ***Cloudy Witness/Blessedly Assured*** portrayed such happenings the reader will be taken even further in the sequel; ***Finding a Happy Medium.***

The saga of three fictional every day couples and their supernatural journeys into the realm of the 'God-kind 'continues.

Main Characters

Etta Mae and Donnie Smith – Bible-thumper & avid golfer

Tonika and Josh Gibbons – The Smith's neighbors

Damien and Delilah (Dee) Whitman – Hedge Fund Advisor & Etta Mae's socialite sister

Stephanie Willis – a fast talking rumor monger and friend of Etta Mae and Tonika

Chapter Six Excerpt

Unbeknownst to Tonika, Etta Mae harbored that very same thought.
"Ex-scu-zze me for a sec, girlfriend!"
Etta Mae rose from her chair and scurried off.
"I'll be right back!"
The bereft young neighbor was left to sort through her own bewildering feelings on the matter.
As a distraction from it all she began flipping through the magazine pages once again.
The bi-racial middle aged woman of Black/German descent had become engrossed in an article when a sudden movement out of the corner of her eye caused the magazine to go flying through the air.
There, standing silently in the center of her friend's kitchen stood a figure of a woman cloaked in darkness.
"Whoa! Oh my God!"
Tonika's heart skipped a hurried beat as she took a sudden intake of breath.
"Who're you an-and wh-what're you doing here?"
Tonika looked long and hard at the intruder. Then suddenly realization hit,
"Ooh no!" Tonika gasped as realization hit. "I-I know who you are!"
The figure remained silent.
The terrified human bolted from her chair and began backing away, preparing to run all while once again taking in the appearance of the specter.
The visible incorporeal spirit was something to behold. The figure was clothed in a black hooded full circle velvet cloak. The foreboding garment obscured the specter's facial features.
Even though a hook and loop mechanism front closure was visible, a slip of red muslin material peaked from beneath the slight opening of the dark cloak.

Her neighbor's home had once again become enshrouded with mystical occurrences. The pungent smell of smoke permeating the room was a huge indication of time spent stirring a cauldron.

"Y-You're that-that wi-witch! You're the Witch of En Dor!"

The cloaked figure remained motionless and silent, neither acknowledging, nor denying the human's startling revelation.

Tonika was still able to screech out a frantic call to her friend even in her state of fear and panic.

"E-Etta! Etta Mae! Gir-rl, you-you really need to get in here!" She yelled. "An-and I mean fast!"

CHAPTER

---

*"The way of a guilty man is crooked,
but as for the pure, his conduct is upright."*
Proverbs 21:8

Ashad, the twelve year old son of Tonika Gibbons jumped down from a white mini-van driven by a soccer mom. Ashad gleefully waved good-bye to his soccer teammate.

The boy's biological father was an American Samoan. The combination of both the child's maternal and paternal genes made for a very handsome adolescent.

"Thanks for the ride, Mrs. Sutton." Ashad said to his friend's mother.

"Hey! Shelton, I'll call you later dude!"

"Okay, dawg! I'll hit you up for a game of "Minecrafts' later!" Shelton yelled out.

"You're on," Ashad yelled. "And don't even think you're getting over my wall dude!"

"Bye, Ashad… tell your mom I said hi!"

The van pulled away filled with laughter as the battle-scarred soccer goalie inserted his key and slowly pushed open the front door.

"Ooh!"

The young boy is startled and confused by seeing his out of commissioned step-father standing in the room.

A messy confrontation earlier between the boy's mom and step-dad days earlier had led to Josh storming out of their home.

"Y-you're home!" The tired twelve year said.

"I-is my mom here?"

Ashad nervously made his way into the kitchen.

"Hello son."

Josh went over to embrace the flustered youngster.

"No, your mom's not home yet, but I think she's on her way."

"Oh… o-kay. I'm just going to go to my room."

But the hasty exit is blocked by Josh's extended arm.

"Wait…wait son… c-can I talk to you for a sec?"

The despondent curly haired adolescent reluctantly obliged the request by tiredly plopping down in a nearby chair. His head remained lowered.

Josh exhaled deeply before beginning to speak.

"Ashad…son, I-I just want to… to apologize to you."

It wasn't an easy task admitting your shortcomings to a twelve year old boy.

The repentant father figure shifted his weight to the edge of the couch.

"I mean f-for disrupting your life these past few days."

Ashad sat listening to the heartfelt words of the man responsible for so much discord in their home.

He didn't know how he was supposed to react to the unusual attention.

The image of seeing his beautiful mother crying suddenly flashed through his young mind.

He had come into the kitchen and found her with her back to him sobbing inconsolably.

His quiet entrance had startled her and she had quickly wiped away tears before turning to embrace him reassuringly by giving him the biggest squishiest bear hug.

Understandably baffled, the question hidden foremost in the lad's mind was how could the man seated next to him readily leave the family he supposedly loved?

"I can understand why everything is confusing to you." Josh went on to say.

"A-all I can tell you is… life has a way of eating you up and spitting you out."

"Huh? O-okay."

Josh reached up and tousled the boy's thick ringlet curls. A deep groan escaped his full lips before he regretfully dropped his hand.

Josh could tell by the confused look on the boy's face he had no clue of what he was saying, or where he was going with their conversation.

"I tell you what little man; let's table this discussion for another time… okay?"

"Okay… Can I go to my room now?"

"That's fine son" Josh grinned. "See you in a bit."

A ton of weights had lifted from the boy's small shoulders.

The boy's face lit up. Flooded with relief, the young man jumped to his feet making way for a hasty retreat.

But instead, Ashad abruptly stopped in mid stride. He suddenly turned to his equally ill-at-ease step-father.

"D-Dad…"

"Yes, son?"

"I-I'm glad you're home."

The tear stained lad ran into his now emotional father's arms. The two held one another for a very long time.

The liberated young man finally pulled free from the unyielding embrace before gleefully running to his room.

Well…one hurdle's down, but then there's that one major hurdle still to come. Josh thought to himself.

Where is she? He wondered. Supposedly she was on her way over an hour ago.

He went over to the front window and peered down the street. The street was empty.

By now, the tall, handsome, athletic built forty year olds' anxiety level is running at an all time high.

"Good grief!"

With little more than showy irritation, the antsy spouse muttered under his breath.

"Even a turtle could've been home by now!"

It didn't help that the head injury he suffered earlier had begun to throb. He was in such pain he went in search of a much needed pain reliever.

That crap happened out of nowhere. He thought on his way to the bathroom.

Josh had been sitting at a red light when two indignant strangers in a black 1990 'Iroc Z' Camaro had pulled up next to his red 2013 Trans Am.

The car's two obnoxious occupants had aggressively challenged the recently rejected suitor to an impromptu race by loudly revving their engine.

It was not something Josh had wanted to do at the time, as an even more pressing matters had been on the rejected amore's agenda.

The whole incident had certainly been a close call. He basically had tried ignoring the villain's ballistic challenge when shots rang out.

Josh was fortunate enough to have escaped the flying bullets with only a graze to his head.

The menacing bandits had then sped off; caring little if any harm had been inflicted on their designed target.

But, what was most intriguing about the whole situation was the aid he had received from a phantom gentleman.

The clandestine figure clad entirely in white had helped the slightly injured man to a nearby bench.

The man showed no concern about his pristine white suit possibly becoming blood stained.

It was also strange was when almost immediately vivid immoral images of Josh's past actions had replayed before his very eyes like a rewinding movie.

He saw himself going to Karla Jordan's, his mistress' apartment to inform her he'd left his wife and son to be with her. He thought she would be elated.

But, once there, the reception he received was a far cry from what the dishonest wooer had expected.

Instead of being met with a loving and caring embrace, the 'mistress from hell's sinister life came into full effect.

Miss Jordan turned out to be a deceptive and manipulative vixen whose sole purpose was to enjoy preying on gullible men's vulnerability.

The dark impulses she looked most favorably upon were breaking up relationships, especially those of married men.

So, true to form, Josh Linden Gibbons, the now defunct athletic apparel entrepreneur had now become her latest victim.

He had fallen prey to a Jezebel spirit disguised as a prominent office executive.

She was a beautiful woman who really turned heads wherever she ventured. Karla also captured men's attention in her revealing mode of dress.

Once Josh had arrived, the shrew had opened her door when the redness of her eyes had sent a shiver down the unsuspecting suitor's spine.

He heard her laugh the most ear piercing shriek. She then commanded he go back to his pitiful family before she slammed the door in his blood drained face.

The deceitfulness of it all was overwhelming. Josh felt the only thing he had left was prayer.

Still shaken while sitting on the bench, he had dropped to his knees and had cried out to God for mercy and forgiveness.

He drew strength from his childhood as he knew there was no shame when you're on your knees.

He'd seen his mother in that posture many times.

Josh remembered the question he asked one day after she had finished praying.

"Why?"

"I humble myself before the Lord." His mother once told him. "It's what He asks us to do. When you kneel, you're in a humbling position. The Lord hears from Heaven when we repent, pray and seek His face when we kneel."

"Why?" He'd repeated.

"Well…" she had answered. "I suppose it's because when we humble ourselves its saying to God we recognize You are bigger; bigger than me, bigger than anyone, or anything!"

The informed back-slider couldn't help but think how kneeling in today's society is thought to be detrimental to the flag and our national anthem.

"If humbleness is all it takes for God to fix this nation," His mother had recently told him, "then I say we should all find ourselves kneeling in prayer!"

She went on to add. "Imagine what would happen if not only athletes, but if the nation as a whole would stop, drop and kneel?"

The repentant adulterer envisioned a jubilant Evelyn Lois Gibbons, his mother, with the most pleasing smile on her face.

Josh had much to pray about and remained on his knees for a length of time.

When next he looked up, the covert gentleman had mysteriously vanished.

But, the mystical rescuer had left behind a renewed and restored human being.

If given the chance, Josh avowed to become the best husband and father deemed possible.

He suddenly jumped up. His mind returned to the present time at hand.

Through his miraculous rejuvenation the young man couldn't wait to share the life changing chance meeting with his devoted wife.

With deep concern weighing heavily on his mind Josh walked over to the front window once again and looked out.

"Come on home baby. Please, just come home!"

CHAPTER

Therefore, since we have so great a cloud of witnesses surrounding us... let us also lay aside every encumbrance and the sin which so easily entangle us, and let us run with endurance the race that is set before us.
Hebrews 12:1 NAS

"**P**ut it off! Put it off right now! Whatever is keeping you from a Spirit–filled life; put it off! And I mean put it off right now!"

"Sto-op! Am I hearing this correctly? That sounds like my father's voice.

After returning from the day's interesting outing and upon entering the luxury suite the commanding voice of his long deceased father reverberated around the room.

The anguished cry proclaimed into the paranormally charged atmosphere was the direct result of a once immoral life style being brought to the fore front.

"No-oo! Make it stop!"

The tormented young New Yorker had retired to his suite after leaving the Smith's home. He had left word for Delilah, his estranged wife to please join him at the Misty Heights Halston Hotel located near the New Jersey airport.

After departing the plane earlier that morning, the Hedge Fund advisor had barely checked in before he was off to the destination that had brought him to the city. He was sure he would fine his wife residing there after her hasty departure.

Oh! He thought. This can only be a carry-over from today at the Smith's home.

"Really, Pops!" Damien declared. As if it wasn't enough to send a desparaging message by way of a phantom, now you are here ranting in my ear!"

Obviously irritated, Damien slammed the car keys down on the veranda with such fury they bounced off and landed on the floor.

"Geez! Old man! Give me a damn break. I've had enough!"

"Whatever is keeping you from serving Jesus, son, I pray you will put it off. Immediately!

The resounding words boomed through the air of the hotel suite with redeeming force.

"Who would believe it?" Damien said aloud. "My dead father's is speaking from the grave just like he's standing right here in this very room!"

The troubled son began pacing the floor, desperately seeking to shut out the intrusive words of the late Rev. J.J. Whitman; Jamison John Whitman.

"My son, run with patience the race that's been set before you."

Grappling fingers reached up to massage pulsing temples.

"Okay! Okay! O-ka-ay! Day-yuum! Would ya' please let up on a brotha!"

It was if he was once again that impressionable young boy standing wide-eyed in the Tabernacle of the Congregation Holiness Church.

Many life changing sermons had come from Rev. Whitman's pulpit enough to last a life time.

Hebrews 12:1 *Therefore, since we are surrounded by such a great cloud of witnesses…"*

It was his father's most preached text.

He thought about how as a youth his mind had deduced the meaning of that text.

So, the way I see it, we're surrounded by dead people who lived victorious lives by believing God and by following His commandments. I believe that's what the scripture is saying. He recalled asking his father if what he thought was correct.

"I guess you could call people like Abraham, Isaac, Jacob, Peter, John, Luke and Mathew saints. I'm pretty sure, if I'm not mistaken they all makeup the cloud of witnesses among others."

He would explain to his congregants in such a way that they soon realized they too will be a part of the spirit realm once they suffer death just as those gone on before us.

Earth is temporary, but heaven and hell is eternal. In fact his exact words were:

"And as it pertains to those witnesses, it would suffice for me to say this world was once also their world; yet, inevitably, their world (heaven), will one day eventually also become our world.

But, the key is in finding that happy medium in the preparation station (earth) through living a holy life down here between now and the hereafter."

Well Pops, Damien thought. You can't help but be a part of that great cloud! Lord knows you've earned it.

I can see you now standing in that 'Hallelujah Square' with open arms looking to greet all your glorified sheep from your pasture down here on earth.

Damien Darnell Smith, a man with usually a calm demeanor stood in the middle of his luxurious hotel suite longing to shut out the intruding voice ringing in his ears.

The luxury hotel reserved the privilege to offer incentives to its high-end clientele.

His room on the first floor had been upgraded to a deluxe suite on the eighth floor.

To say the bank executive's response to the upgrade was anything but exuberant would be an oxymoron.

Damien threw up both his hands in defeat as he became more despondent over the whole fiasco.

As a former preacher's kid in small-town Georgia, Damien now found himself at a crossroads in life.

"I surrender! Pops, did you hear me?" He shouted. "I surrender it all! It's not like you don't already know. I know you heard my prayer at the Smith's home today. Don't you get it; I've already surrendered!"

Rather than conforming to the 'rule of thumb' per se' through the years the yearling heir had chosen to navigate through life on his own merits.

The former 'PK' had become a non-conformist in his adult life. He no longer practiced Christianity.

But, be that as it may, a paradigm shift had happened after finally submitting to the divine cajoling.

Damien now knew without question what it was he truly needed to do. He now knew he needed to 'put off' any and all burden baring obstacles keeping him from his calling.

There could be no other way. Now ready to comply, he was suddenly engulfed with a flood of precious memories.

"Yes, Rev. Whitman, you did it your way." He said aloud. "And… so now I'm left to do my will and do it my way."

The sound of hearty laughter off in the distance stopped the errant son dead in his tracks.

"Yes, it's true; I'm not going to lie. I did make a mess of things. But, I'm a new creation in Christ Jesus now!"

The redeemed soul thought long and hard before saying what came next.

"B-but with you, Pops, as my sole witness, I vow to make it all right again."

Even with all that being said, melancholy symptoms hung heavily on his shoulders as he once again paced the floor.

The man's dire situation may prove to be too overwhelming for even the staunchest believers.

What's up with all this supernatural shit happening to me today anyway? He thought. Lately, I've been talking with the dead like I'm talking with my clients.

"Who does that?"

And then a certain man's face came to mind.

"That darn Donnie Leroy Smith that's who!"

Just the thought of the earlier scenario frayed his nerves.

"I knew there was something weird about that man when I first laid eyes on him."

Damien couldn't help but think how his high end clients would react knowing somehow between leaving my home and arriving in this God-forsaken city I've somehow have become a freaking medium! I talk to dead people.

"He sees and talks to dead people!" He could fathom a future client saying.

"And I the hell don't want some unbalanced, Italian suit wearing savvy psychopathic kook sanctioning any of my hard earned coins!"

If the ice gray walls of the luxury hotel suite could talk he was sure they could tell of the revealing secrets now being laid out before him.

Damien cleared the credulous thought from his mind by unwittingly taking stock of his surroundings.

The hotel suite was high glamour all the way, but was yet subtle enough for even the most macho of men to feel at ease.

The luxury suite's paint palette was strongly complimented by the metallic gray tufted couch and chair accented by mirrored coffee and end tables.

The plush white wool carpet was no less for wear, considering the constant pacing it endured by the nineteen hundred dollar Ferragomo crocodile loafers worn by its current occupant.

But, even though he was accustomed to the finer things in life, the opulent surroundings did little to soothe the frayed nerves of the shirtless Adonis as he stood clad only in Italian slacks and shoes.

Just days earlier he recalled how following a heated argument, his wife Delilah with suit cases in hand had abruptly left their New York apartment.

Had it not been for the possibility of having a civil conversation with his agitated spouse had he checked into the posh ten story hotel in the first place.

Ironically, at the time he hadn't hindered her hurried departure. But, in the days that followed the distraught spouse was feeling his wife's absence.

After overcoming a scarred ego Damien soon realized the amount of love he still had for Delilah was as strong as when they first met.

The distraught banker sat in deep though with his mind replaying the course of the past year or so.

When he and Delilah Carol first met she had been a recent divorced socialite.

In fact, the curt petite olive skinned damsel had been married to two or three prominent older gentlemen before. The marriages had either ended in death, or in divorce.

He himself was ten years her junior when they had married. By marrying the young banker the well established socialite had broken from her questionable tradition.

But, in this case, age certainly didn't matter, because the awe struck suitor couldn't help but fall in love with the high class beauty.

The impeccably dressed vixen's effervescent spirit had drawn the savvy young suitor like a giant magnet.

He spied her standing alone with drink in hand one night at a gala event, and the rest is history.

As the favorable memories of that night flooded his mind, Damien knew now more than ever he was not ready to give up on their union.

Not even after fully knowing the outcome of it all fully rested on his wife's unmerited and undeserved forgiveness; could he even think about giving up.

Surely by now Delilah had cooled off a bit. He thought. Surely they could talk it out; right? Their future depended on it.

The day she left, Damien knew the only place she would run to was to an older sister.

So, with hopeful reconciliation in the forefront, the determined optimist had boarded a flight and followed his wife to Chauncey, New Jersey, a small bedroom community of about 55,000 residents.

Albeit, on the car ride to his in-laws home, the subdued traveler's mood swung wildly from somber optimistic to that of complete desperation.

Damien soon realized just how farfetched it would appear to meet his in-laws today after never having done so in the past.

A justifiable, he reasoned, was that a hectic work schedule prevented the Hedge-fund investor from ever docking the Smith's door in the established years of their marriage.

But, however, he had spoken with the sister, Etta Mae Smith over the phone a time or two. And she had seemed pleasant enough.

Still, the uncertainty of the outcome of this trip was proving to be a bit much. He was becoming weary in the pursuit of a possible reconciliation.

"Today's been a beast! No! I take that back; the whole damn week's been a freaking beast!"

Once he had arrived at his destination and after casually checking his appearance in the rental car's rear view mirror, he had exited the vehicle.

He had taken several deep breaths before approaching the oak paneled front door. He had rang the bell.

The door had flown open and the anxious pursuer was met face to face with a thin, slightly balding, tall humorous man with skin the color of cocoa. He had met Donnie LeRoy Smith.

Even though he had tried calming his jittery nerves, the moment the door had flown open Damien's life was never the same from that point on.

The unstoppable dynamo had brushed past the startled home owner like a freight train racing down a track with the sole purpose of seeking his wife.

"Delilah!" The over anxious pursuer had called out her name a number of times. Delilah! Delilah!"

The over wrought homeowner had looked with amazement at the flagrant intruder.

"Is my wife here?"

Donnie could only guess the invading tyrant barging into his home could only be his sister-in-law's errant spouse.

"Whoa! Hold on there now big fellow! Donnie had cautioned. "I think you'd better slow your roll. You don't own nuthin' up in here."

Donnie had tried at first without much success in restraining the charging bull.

But, it wasn't long afterward; after gaining his composure, when what could've been a volatile situation was finally under control.

The two greenhorns had talked at length before finally becoming comfortable with each other's presence.

Damien's current distress was only heightened upon discovering that neither his wife nor her sister was available.

But the connecting factor which really brought the two together was when seemingly out of nowhere unexplainable happenings had begun to manifest.

A "close encounter of the paranormal kind" had made itself known.

Donnie, the unsuspecting host, had said he felt as if he had somehow become a cast member in a 'pop-up video.'

But that the strange occurrences weren't too surprising however, as he'd just witnessed an alarming episode earlier that morning before showering.

Donnie had also told him how he had inadvertently stumbled upon a biblical specter in the form of *Eve*, "the mother of all living" right there in his own home.

There she stood he had said having a verbal conversation with Etta Mae and Tonika Gibbons, their neighbor as if it was perfectly normal.

Damien had chuckled when he heard how the woman's unsettling appearance had caused Donnie to pee his pants. Even now the unimaginable scene bought much needed laughter in his being.

Still later, that same apparition had reappeared to he and Damien accompanied by her spouse, *Adam*.

It would seem the man *Adam* had been in search of his wandering spouse, his 'help meet.'

To Donnie's amazement, *Adam* had also delivered a message from the beyond to Damien his befuddled houseguest.

"Let me out of here! This is some crazy shit!"

Damien had shouted during the strange occurrence.

The frightened man had brushed past Donnie only to be stopped by *Adam*.

"*Oh, don't bother Brother Man; it is for that you I've really come.*"

The incomparable scene was extremely overwhelming to say the least as Damien asked the question.

"Y-You came for me? Why? What did I do?"

Now thinking back on it, Damien could only see the irony of it all.

""I have come to tell you young man,

that neither the Heavenly Father, nor your earthly father is pleased with how your life has gone."

In fact, the Father's not too particularly pleased with the way the whole world has gone!"

Then after a brief moment a remorseful messenger thought to add.

"Unfortunately, I'm the culprit; it's all my fault. It's all due to my disobedience; me, yours truly. Oh, and of course her; my wife, my help meet.

"You ain't even lied!" Donnie had blurted out.

He chuckled as he blatantly asked what exactly had bought the apparitions to his dwelling.

"But, you said you came for Bro' Man here, remember; so, what do you have for my main man?"

The so called Bro-Man was visibly shaken.

The whole time, he remembered feeling as if the very breath had been knocked from his very core.

In the full scheme of things, the awe-struck recipient thought of the message as something beyond comprehension.

It was at that exact moment he had seen his life as having been an acute lie.

He had soon come to realize that his sexual orientation had come under attack through 'the enemy.'

It was then the repenting Damien had fallen to his knees and had offered up the most soul wrenching prayer he'd ever prayed in his life. He had felt his prayer had shaken the courts of heaven.

Now the 'blood bought' redeemed Holy Ghost filled convert desperately sought and needed his wife's forgiveness even more so.

In the end the wearied optimist could only hope God's favor would act on his behalf.

CHAPTER

Above all, love one another earnestly,
since love covers a multitude of sins.
1 Peter 4:8

"Sister, are you sure you want to do this?" Etta Mae asked Delilah. "I mean

"Don't do that Etta!" Dee shouted. "My mind is already a ball of confusion, so I don't need you to add to it!"

Then with a less agitated tone, the perplexed sister said more apologetically.

"Believe me, I appreciate all your concern, but, this is something I feel in my heart that I must do."

Deep silence enveloped the car as the stressed siblings are locked in their own fretful thoughts.

One is thinking on what to expect with what lies ahead. Etta Mae's mind can't shake the uncertainties awaiting her beloved sister.

It was all Etta Mae Smith could do to keep from restraining her headstrong sister from exiting her gray sedan.

She already knew any effort on her part would be pointless as Dee was a woman who always knew what she wanted, and nothing could stop her once her mind was made up.

Knowing this, even though she was deeply concerned the elder sister kept her futile thoughts private.

After all, the reasoning behind her sister's unseasonable visit only added fuel to the complex episode.

Earlier that morning, Dee had made it perfectly clear she wasn't ready to discuss the matter of her current marriage with anyone.

But, always the doting mother-hen, Etta Mae brooded over the fact she may have just released her sister to cope with a most unfavorable situation alone.

She knew there to be trouble in the marriage, but to what extent, she didn't have a clue.

But, be that as it may, all marriages she reasoned have their ups and downs. Maybe I'm just over dramatizing. Etta Mae thought.

After all, who better knows what's needed at the time than those who're actually involved.

Sometimes separation is the best thing, and if not, well, only time will tell.

In any case, I'm here if she needs me; as always.

The words of her beloved grandmother flooded her memory.

Grams, as she lay dying had said to her. "My dear Etta, always be a 'rock in a weary land' for your sisters as I've tried to be for each of you."

But, at the moment, concern and worry were chipping away at that rock.

Well, Grams," She said aloud. "It hasn't been easy, but Lord knows I've tried.

The corners of her mouth etched into a somber smile as she thought of the promise she'd made decades ago.

Suddenly, the bleating sound of a blaring car horn broke into her solemn thoughts.

Bo-oomp! Bo-ooomp! Boo-oomp!

The startled daydreamer jumped just out of shear panic. Her over correcting sent the car into a collision with the curbside.

Her quick action avoided a collision with the red Hyundai Sonata.

The car's irate driver at the moment was exuding the very essence of road-rage.

"Crimey, woman do I have to drive for the two of us? Stay in your damn lane!"

The middle aged driver with a shock of red hair yelled through his partially rolled down window.

"What world are you driving in? He continued.

"Enough already!" Etta Mae shouted, while frantically rolling down her car window.

The peeved driver met the equally miffed woman's snide remark with an inflamed finger gesture followed with highly charged expletives before racing off.

"Lord Jesus! Take the wheel!"

"On top of all I've been through today. Now comes this nitwit!"

Erratic heartbeats soon normalized as she sat thinking.

"I just dropped my sister off to God knows what! For all I know that Damien could be a plumb psychopath!"

She proceeded to pick up her cell phone while her car is still parked beside the road.

The Android device suffered little damage as she pointedly punched each familiar digit.

As her justifiable rant continued, she glanced over her shoulder looking for a safe path back into the flow of traffic.

You never know these days, but Lord help 'im if he so much as to lay a hand on my sister. She thought as she placed the phone to her ear.

"Umph, I can tell you the earth won't be big enough for the scoundrel to hide in!" She shouted aloud.

With a careful check over her left shoulder the grey 2000 Audi S4 merged into traffic just as a familiar tenor voice came on the line.

A ringing cell phone sent Donnie LeRoy Smith into a frantic search for the newly acquired Samsung Galaxy 8 cell phone before he finally located it.

"H-Hello?"

He breathlessly said into the phone.

"Oh! Hi hun!"

The slimly built slightly balding landscaper and avid golfer said into the phone.

On the other end of the receiver was Etta Mae, his wife.

"What'z—

Deeply concerned, Donnie plopped down on a kitchen stool and out of habit nervously began to rub his bald spot.

"Etta! Are you alright?"

The troubled listener plugged an ear to drown out distracting noises in an effort to hear his clearly hysterical wife more clearly.

"Honey please slow down." He gently instructed. "You're rambling on so I can't understand what you are saying.'

He listened for a moment with genuine concern. After hearing of her close call with another car, he exhaled a sigh of relief.

"Oh, thank God you weren't hurt."

Donnie was able to relax a bit and listened more intently on her reasoning for being in such a predicament.

"She actually went there, huh?" He said unbelievingly.

So, the two sisters were able to meet up after both having gone their separate ways earlier that day. There was something mystical about it all he thought.

"I'm glad you were in the right place at the right time." He said.

His wife had gone shopping, and Dee had left hours later for a walk around the neighborhood, apparently to clear her head.

Donnie had expected either of the two women to return home way before any action was taken on behalf of dealing with Damien.

He could sense his wife's discomfort and concern for her sister's well being, so he said to her.

"Honey, I tell you what; why don't you come on home so we can talk about this? Okay?"

He wiped a bead of sweat from his forehead with the back of his hand.

"I know. I-I know honey." He said into the receiver after listening a bit longer.

It sounds like we've both had a crazy day, s-so hurry home."

A moment of so passed before he added. "Okay, see you soon then. Okay, bye-bye."

Donnie's mind raced as he punched the off-button. His usually calm nerves were on end due to the strange happenings of the past couple of days.

Instinctively, he glanced over at his golf clubs, thinking a round of golf would be what the doctor ordered. Surely hitting a ball or two could soothe his troubling mind.

No. Not today. He thought. I'll sit this one out and wait for Etta Mae. His mind drifted back to where it all began.

Delilah Whitman, or Dee as Etta Mae called her sister, lived in New York for most of her adult life. But, a few days ago, the regal socialite had unexpectedly showed up at their door.

Even though his wife had been somewhat surprised at the timing of her sister's sudden appearance, it was not alarming.

Apparently, Delilah Carol Collins Melvin Cox Jefferson Whitman, had a history of doing the unexpected.

She was currently situated in her fourth marriage. Donnie could only chuckle as he recalled the many antics his wife had told of her sister's fast paste life.

He knew Delilah to be the middle sister out of three girls.

The youngest sibling, Cynthia lived in Charville, North Carolina, and had most recently graduated from a theological seminary there.

She now served as an associate minister with a major congregation in Charville.

Etta Mae, now retired from nursing, and a self proclaimed bible-thumper in her own rite, had only hoped her baby sister had found the answer to her most troubling question; "why do bad things happen to good people?"

It was a burning quest Cynthia had long sought the answer to after losing their parents in an airline tragedy.

Grams, their beloved paternal grandmother took on the task of rearing the sisters during their formative years.

But, as was the case, Etta Mae, the oldest, had solemnly promised their dying grandmother she would carry the torch as acting matriarch.

The task alone was a major undertaking. Donnie chuckled aloud. He thought of how proud he felt of his wife, just thinking how loyal she had been in carrying out her duties.

Even now, he thought, her home was still a place of refuge.

But, he found it troubling how even after being with her sister for a couple of days how Dee had never shared with Etta Mae the exact circumstances.

He thought of how just today she had even divulged a minute sketch of her troubles in a roundabout way even to him.

How would her meeting with Damien play out? He wondered.

Donnie recalled how Damien, had shown up unexpected frantically searching for his missing wife.

Then finally, after much evening mayhem and discussion, Damien had asked him to inform Delilah of his whereabouts before leaving.

Donnie was eager to share the evening's escapades with Delilah and was hopeful she would return from her walk before his wife's shopping trip was over.

But, apparently, that had not been the case. Donnie had promptly called Etta Mae and had informed her of what had transpired. Not knowing Dee was already in her company.

Ummph! Looks like 'ole girl' got the message.

He thought after learning his wife had delivered her sister to the hotel Damien had indicated.

"I wonder how it's all going to go down!"

He had just mumbled this under his breath when he caught a sudden movement of his stealthy adversary crouching in his back yard.

Donnie leaned forward and as always, it set his blood to boiling.

"Damn it! I just ran that scoundrel out of my yard a few hours ago! Now he's back again! Still after my Japanese Koi!"

The Smith's home was a well-kept ranch situated on a tree-lined residential street.

The living room - dining room combination layout consisted of a makeup of contemporary décor.

Two brown love seats of a very fine grain of leather sat facing each other divided by a square mahogany coffee table.

The room further featured bold designs, with bright colors, and innovative materials with two floral patterned occasional chairs sitting in respective corners.

An array of family portraits and other mementos sat pristinely on a mahogany sofa table behind one of the love seats.

The same color scheme flowed into the dining area. The dark mahogany buffet and dining table with four chairs sat on a brown/gold Oriental rug.

"Oh, no you don't! Not again!"

He yelled, bolting through the back door, but not before stopping to grab an old nine iron.

With adrenaline pumping, the infuriated home owner swung into action.

Donnie was determined no fish stealing, catnip loving feline was going to rob him of his hard won labor of achievement.

That Koi pond was his pride and joy. He'd spent time, money and labor on the beloved project.

It even took him away from his beloved golf game.

As if sensing the impending danger, with one white booted paw poised in midair, the object of the man's rage stopped dead in its tracks.

The parti-colored brown-white and gold Calico cat met his attacker's rage with a wide-eyed stare.

Completely oblivious to the impending danger brightly hued Japanese Koi swam lazily in their beautifully constructed pond.

"You thieving ball of fur!" Donnie shouted. "I just chased you out of my yard an hour ago; now here you are again.

The enraged pond owner tripped as he stepped from the porch.

"Damn!" He said as he righted himself.

The man-made pond was surrounded by an abundance of colorful plants and flowers. The pond was the homeowners pride and joy.

Donnie thought he had taken all the precautionary measures necessary to keep his prized pond safe from roaming varmints.

As a plant lover, the fledgling horticulturist had once read how the plant Coleus Canina was good in keeping cats away when planted as a hedge around gardens and landscaped areas.

The plant produces an odor when cats rub against the leaves. The rubbing act causes the cats grave discomfort.

But, it seemed even though he had done so, this one vermin had somehow become immune to the plant's effect.

It only took a second before the startled would be rogue feline sped off and bolted threw a hole in the neighbor's fence.

"You had you better go!"

Donnie turned around headed back to the house still mumbling under his breath.

"I can tell you this; no Sushi will be on your diet tonight buddy! Not on my watch!"

The irate homeowner stopped to catch his breath after the stress induced jaunt.

"And don't you even dare think about coming back, you piece of-

"No-oo!" A trembling little voice shouted over the fence.

"Mr. Donnie, don't hurt my friend!"

Donnie, still fuming, eyes were instantly drawn to short brown scrawny legs hooked over a Jungle Gym.

Primed for a confrontation, the little pixie with hands clenched in fists angrily rushed to the neighbor's fence.

The now deflated neighbor couldn't help but chuckle at the noticeable toothless gap of his little wide-eyed adversary.

Death defying darts was being shot from non-other than ten year old McKenzie Lauren Reid; affectionately known as 'Mac.'

McKenzie was John and Kathy Reid's youngest daughter. The older daughter, Mikaela was a senior in high school, and would soon be graduating and heading off to college.

The high tech couple's favorite joke would often be about the eight year gap between the two girls.

"Thanks to our little hatchling," they would always say. "Our nest is anything but empty."

The Reid's and Smiths had been neighbors for well over twenty years. Donnie could easily recall each of the girl's birth.

"Uh, Umm!" Clearing his throat, Donnie addressed the defiant little vixen. "Oh!' Hi there Mac… I didn't see you over there."

The visibly agitated youngster stood with her arms folded and feet firmly planted apart. All while keeping a watchful eye locked on her six-foot nemesis.

Donnie could hear her heavy breathing, but he also saw tears forming in her eyes.

McKenzie Lauren Reid, the pint sized 'defender of stray felines' tucked her long micro braided hair firmly behind pierced ears adorned with little crosses.

To Donnie, the child's troubling demeanor was quite amiable.

The now flushed caramel colored face with a smudge was moist with little beads of sweat.

The child definitely had her father's chiseled face that featured high cheek bones. Dark brown eyes peered out from naturally curled lashes.

Donnie thought how the little snub nose and perky lips made the little spitfire the very essence of cuteness.

"Mr. Donnie!" She was finally able to say. "Please don't kill Miss Gretchen's kitty cat!"

"I-I wasn't trying to." Donnie stammered.

"Yes you were. I saw you."

She was right. Had he made contact with the little nuisance the outcome would've be catastrophic.

"Miss Gretchen got lots of cats and they–

"Well, he needs to stay out of my yard."

Donnie cut the little whipper-snapper off with his own declaration.

"And if I catch that cat around my Koi pond again, I'll-

"She's not a he, she's a she!"

Mac stated emphatically as she defiantly folded her arms once again.

"She-he!" Donnie shot back. "Who the heck cares?"

Then after thinking he added. "And how would you know?"

What level have I stooped to? He thought. I can't believe I'm caught up in a war of words with this little munchkin.

"Because she has kittens and they're right over there."

But the war raged on. Mac hurriedly pointed to an area near the far end of the fence.

Donnie's unbelieving eyes followed the direction she was pointing.

Lo' and behold! He spotted the mother cat with what seem to be a brood of four kittens.

A tear stained face solemnly turned to look at the perplexed man standing before her.

Donnie felt a pang of remorse especially after seeing the child's little lips quivering.

"I'm sorry Mac." He apologetically said.

"Now that I know the cat's a mother, Miss Gretchen's bunch of fur balls is safe with me."

"Oh! Thank you! Thank you Mr. Donnie!

Childlike exuberance replaced the once hostile demeanor.

"And I know Mr. Donnie how much you love your fishes." She stated.

"Yes, I do love my fish." Donnie emphasized. "Not my fishes."

"Huh?" McKenzie asked with the cutest childlike curiosity.

"Never mind, Mac." He said.

Donnie couldn't help but giggle. The little pixie was right. Even though he loved golfing, landscaping was something the homeowner prided himself on doing well.

"So, the mama cat has kittens, huh?"

"Yes!" Mac excitedly replied. "I pet them all the time. I like the silver tabby best."

She then thought to offer a solution to both their problems.

"He-ey! Mr. Donnie!"

"Yes, Mackenzie."

"I know what!"

"You know?" And just what is it you know, young lady?"

"My dad can fix that hole!" The young whipper-snapper answered, hardly able to contain her excitement.

"Th-enn!"

"Then what?"

"The momma cat can't eat your fish!"

The innocent peace offering bought a smile to the prized pond owner's face.

Donnie unsuccessfully muffled a chuckle as he mulled over the child's ready solution.

"Hmmmm... well...I tell you what Mac." Donnie said.

"What, Mr. Donnie?" The girl asked with a bright expectant smile.

"On the condition you make darn sure that cat and her brood stays on your side of the fence!"

"Oh! Promise, I promise!" McKenzie said gleefully jumping up and down. "The momma cat will stay!"

"A-and, I also think you had better talk with your dad before you go signing him up for added chores."

"Ooops! One small hand flew up to cover her mouth as she snickered. "I'll ask my dad tonight when he gets home, Mr. Donnie."

Just the thought of her feline friends were no longer in harm's way had given the elated child an adrenalin rush.

Before her adversary, but once again friendly neighbor could say anything, McKenzie did a full back flip.

Mac had become an agile little gymnast for her short years in gymnastics.

"Oh! What bought that on? I didn't expect all that!"

Secretly, the relieved neighbor was as equally happy their respectable friendship had been reestablished. But he wasn't about to do any summersaults.

The two co-conspirators laughed heartedly. Mac returned once again to the fence.

"Okay, little Mac, lets pinky-swear. You'll keep the Calico fur ball away from my fish pond. Ri-ight?"

He offered her his pinky finger over the fence. It was received with the biggest grin that also revealed yet another missing tooth she'd recently lost.

Skepticism was next on the agenda.

"Pinky swear? Mr. Donnie what'z a pinky swear?"

"Oh, I'm sorry darling. I should've known you didn't know what I was talking about."

He then went on to explain his offer.

"A *pinky promise,* or a '*pinky swear*' is when two people hook little fingers together like this. Then they make an agreement."

"Oo-oh! I get it."

A look of understanding came over the innocent face.

"Koo-ool" But then she looked questionably at her little finger.

But... Mr. Donnie... my little finger isn't pink and neither is yours. So..."

The amused neighbor roared with laughter. Oh, to have the innocence of a child. He thought.

"No, little munchkin, our pinkies are not pink. They're brown. What I said is all just a figure of speech."

He thought for a minute before offering a solution.

"I tell you what Mac. Since your finger is brown, and my finger is brown; let's just 'brownie swear!"

"Yeah! I can brownie swear! Let's brownie swear."

The elated youngster seemed hard pressed trying to contain the excitement over their secret pact.

Soon brown fingers entwined together in agreement as the highly impressionable novice and amused neighbor repeated their pledge.

"Now then McKenzie." Donnie said afterwards calling his partner in crime by her full name. "I'm going to hold you to it."

"I won't let you down, Mr. Donnie. The smiling child declared. "You can count on me!

"Well, okay then Mac. See to it."

He turned to leave the giggling youngster fully knowing it was little chance in hell the rogue feline could be kept out of his yard.

"Mc-ken-zie!"

Kora Reid called from the open door of her home. "It's time for you to come in, honey."

"Mac... now stop pestering Mr. Smith. The concerned mother waved at her neighbor.

"Coming, Mommy... bye Mr. Donnie!"

And as she ran, the rambunctious little spitfire did a full cartwheel before reaching her mother's waiting arms. Mrs. Reid reached out to embrace her daughter in a tight squeeze.

"Honey, now be careful. Don't step in a mole hole. Your dad has his work cut out for himself."

The concerned parent took her eye off her little firecracker long enough to wave to her neighbor once again.

Donnie stood watching the loving camaraderie between the mother and daughter being played out before him.

Mental scenes of his wife and Janet, their only daughter during her formative years flashed through his mind. Janet was now a fully fledged pediatrician whose practice kept her busy in the great state of Hawaii.

Her husband Geoffrey was a general practitioner in the same hospital. The father's only regret was the couple had put off having children far too long.

Oh, if only I could become a granddaddy. He thought.

Unlike his wife, who had simply resolved never to pressure the couple in their decision making was something that weighed heavily on his mind.

So much so, he would casually slip in the question each time Janet would call.

"When am I going to become a grandfather?"

And as always, the question would simply be met with the usual laughter and a "Oh, daddy."

"Well hello, Donnie!"

Kora's greeting snapped the daydreamer out of his daze back into reality.

"I hope my little 'Denise the Menace' wasn't bothering you too much."

"Oh! Hi Kora and no, Mac was no bother at all. In fact, she was a very big help."

"Oh!" Well alright then. I know my little jumping bean can be a bit much at times so…"

Once again the smiling mother squeezed her daughter tightly before turning to leave.

"See you later, Donnie! Tell Etta Mae I said hi!"

"I'll be sure to do that Kora. See ya' later! Take care."

As he was making his way to the house he heard a car pull into the garage. An anxious husband went in search of his frantic and distressed wife, eager to hear all about her day.

CHAPTER
Four

> ⁵*Trust in the Lord with all your heart and*
> *lean not on your own understanding;*
> ⁶*in all your ways submit to him,*
> *and he will make your paths straight.*
> **Proverbs 3:5-6(NIV)**

"Well Lord," the distraught husband cried out. "My life is certainly in your hands now, so it's all up to you."

The wearied soldier remained in deep thought. A minute or two went by before he became instantly aware of his attire.

Damien did not care to be presumptuous although it would be his own wife he would be meeting.

I can't assume anything or take anything for granted at this point and time. He thought. He slipped comfortably into the plush monogrammed robe provided by the hotel.

After pouring himself a drink of Cognac he ventured over to the window and peered out the pewter gray European jacquard drapes.

Suddenly, down below in the parking lot Damien spied the object of his unrest exiting a grey luxury sedan.

His heart pounded in his chest like a bass drum in a marching band as he lowered his tensed body into a tufted Barrel Armchair.

"And so the games begin." He uttered with uneasiness. "Lord, where do I go from here? I need you to hold my hand."

Generalized anxiety can blossom into full-blown panic when faced with uncertainties. It's a given.

Considering the predicament she now faced, Delilah Whitman knew this all too well.

The thought of what lie ahead in just a few minutes were enough to bring even the most docile maiden to a breaking point.

But, despite it all, she accepted the open door respectfully being held open by a tall blond, robust, ruddy cheek doorman. She noticed the man's eyes were pools of blue.

"Thank you, sir."

"You're welcome, madam."

The doorman smiled and looked away. Newly determined and deliberate steps now carried the nervous-Nellie into the swank hotel lobby.

The New York socialite had resolved to grab the 'bull by the horns' today unlike in days past.

What will it be; an inconclusive, perhaps or a conclusive ending to all this?

Delilah asked herself as she approached the hotel's raised granite counter.

It was the least she could do, she concluded, considering the enlightening wisdom that had been poured into her confused mind earlier.

"And that's the only reason I'm here!" She spoke into the air.

Delilah was greeted by an impeccably dressed concierge standing erect at the front of the counter with a ready built smile plastered on his face.

A young and perky desk assistant stood smiling behind the counter.

As she approached, the slender brunette assistant slowly turned directing her attention to sorting through loose papers laying on a nearby credenza.

The intended slight hadn't gone unnoticed by Delilah as she addressed the well rehearsed smile of the concierge now greeting her with an extended hand.

"Hello, madam." The concierge said with an imposed English persona while taking a full sweep of her person.

"May I assist you in any way?"

The slight quiver in the woman's voice betrayed the calm demeanor she was hoping she portrayed.

"H-hello, I'm here to meet my husband. M-may I have M-Mr. Damien Whitman's suite, please?"

But what began as a seemingly innocent request was met instead with a collective gasp and unbelievably wide-eyed stares.

The overall reaction of both he and the assistant was a bit deflating to say the least. Delilah stood frozen with a puzzled look on her face.

"I'm sorry," she finally was able to say, "but is there a problem?"

As a New York socialite herself, Delilah was well aware of the major policies upscale hotels carried.

She had certainly been guests as well as hosts to some of New York's finest gala gatherings in such hotels.

She was well aware of the fact, in order to increase the level of personal relationships with guests, such hotels front desks and concierge services often acted as a single host.

So, she concluded, judging by the assistant's reaction to her entry, the lone host, being the concierge was there to answer any and all her questions.

Knowing this, Delilah was now becoming a bit miffed at both their attitudes toward her.

The awkward moment was soon recovered by the concierge's taunt response.

"I'm sorry, Madam," he said with implied emphasis. "As much as it would please me to assist you, it is not this hotel's policy to disclose our guest registry to strangers."

"Not your policy!" The agitated inquirer shouted a decibel over normal.

"Then how pray tell did you not just hear me say I was here to see-my-husband!"

The startled slim brunette looked up sharply from her papers before abruptly walking away.

It never ceases to amaze me, the rudeness of some people. She thought.

The once demure concierge sensing an impending confrontation extended a peace offering.

"I'm sorry madam," he said with resilience. "If you care to show some form of ID... perhaps I could better assist you."

He had noticed the woman upon entering had not carried a purse. But, he had noticed her attire was that to which the hotel's clientele was most accustomed.

The ball was now in her court. She glanced through the doors and noticed the doorman observing the scene.

But she was at a loss as she had left her sister's home hours earlier not bothering to take her purse.

Besides, she little expected to find herself standing in a luxurious hotel inquiring about the whereabouts of Mr. Damien Darnell Whitman.

With that being the case, there was no way she could possibly identify herself.

Delilah thought for a moment before mischievously placing her left hand on the speckled gray counter. She took note of his name on the brass nametag. Feeling devious, Delilah coyly asked.

"Ah... Pi-erre's is it?"

"Yes, madam."

"I don't think you understand."

An impressionable demeanor overtook the young man's expression.

Delilah smiled. She was highly pleased with the reaction to her cunning plot.

Pierre's gaze had become fixed on the object making too loud of a statement to be ignored.

"I know my husband has a suite in this hotel. So... if you would kindly 'ring' his room and..."

"Uh, humm," I see madam."

He looked once again at the huge rock adorning the well-manicured tapered fingers before proceeding to check his registry.

"I'm sorry, and his name again?"

"Damien, a Mr. Damien Whitman."

"Thank you."

Delilah smiled with renewed confidence.

"Yes, madam, I'm ringing his suite now."

Satisfied with her success, only then with a sigh of relief, did she begin to take note of her opulent surroundings. She too could appreciate the finer things in life.

Delilah took in the unique and stylish motorized roller blinds encasing the aluminum floor to ceiling windows.

Dark mahogany paneling worthy of any five star venues enveloped the lobby in richness.

Exotic green plants rising from ornate hammered copper pots sat well situated in strategic areas.

Taupe high back duchess arm chairs constructed from the finest calf's leather was arrayed throughout the lobby in conversational groupings.

Well done Mr. Whitman. She thought. I knew you wouldn't have it any other way.

A smug smile spread across her face in spite of the gnawing feelings of doubt resting deep in her gut.

"Ah, yes, Mr. Whitman, I'm sorry sir, but there's a…" He said, throwing an inquiring glance at the stranger standing before him.

"I'm sorry madam… your name?"

"Oh, yes, yes of course. It's Delilah," She emphatically stated.

"Delilah Whitman."

"A Mrs. Delilah Whitman is here to speak with you sir." The flustered young man said into the phone.

"Yes… yes sir, I'll send her right up. Yes, thank you sir."

With mission accomplished the frayed nerves intensified. Could she go through with this? She wondered.

Could she look the betrayer of their marriage vows squarely in the face?

The concierge's direct stare brought Delilah's mind back to the matter at hand.

"Ma-dam, Mr. Whitman, uh mm, your husband," he respectfully said, "is expecting you. You will find him in Suite 805 on the eighth floor."

Satisfied with himself for offering such pristine service he came from behind the desk and directed the self-willed guest to her destination.

"Madam, the elevators are just ahead to your left. And have a good day."

Having said all there was to say he then went behind the desk and turned his attention to the computer screen.

Feeling abruptly dismissed Delilah politely thanked Pierre for his service and sauntered over to the stainless steel and baked enamel double door elevator.

Alone in the ornamental enclosure, she asked herself even more questions.

She even fleetingly allowed a brief moment to calm raging nerves as her hands had begun shaking uncontrollably.

All too soon, with the sound of a ding, indicating the elevator had reached the eighth floor, the ornate doors slid open.

Delilah stepped out into the hallway and slowly walked in the direction the arrow indicated to find Room 805.

Any moment now, with the turn of a knob, she would look into the shameful eyes that had caused her the most unbearable pain.

But, as she stood there in the hallway, ironically, the fleeting moment soon passed.

The moment was overwhelmingly replaced with a sense of calmness. Shock had been her first emotion, but it had quickly been followed by a sense of anticipation.

That once dreadful incident no longer had her seething with rage as it once did.

What's up with that… She wondered. What's happened to me?

All too soon Delilah found herself standing before Suite 805.

Nervously, she lifted her hand to knock on the door, but allowed it to drop once again to her side.

In an effort to squelch the uncontrollable trembling, Delilah clenched both hands in a tight fist.

Then, finally after deeply exhaling she raised her knuckles tapping lightly on the solid oak door.

But, to her amazement, even before the first knock was sounded, the suite's door flew open.

"H-hello, Delilah. I-"

Damien extended a slightly shaking hand as he was unsure of her reactions.

To her surprise, Delilah found herself brushing aside the extended hand, but instead flung herself into her husband's strong familiar arms.

The once estranged couple embraced for a length of time before Delilah lifted her lips and received a sweet succulent kiss.

Then in one swift swoop her petite frame was lifted from the floor and carried over the threshold.

Damien kicked the door close with one foot as the passion which once existed between the two was once again rekindled as a burning fire.

Forgiveness is a strange bed-fellow. They each thought.

CHAPTER

For all have sinned, and come short of the glory of God; Being justified freely by his grace through the redemption that is in Christ Jesus:
Romans 3:23-26 AV

I now have a new friend. A jubilant Tonika, the biracial was part German and African American whose ancestry hailed from the Rhineland Pfalz region in Germany.

Apparently, the mother of one thought. Delilah had had a "come to Jesus" meeting with a Prophet Cummings on her afternoon walk.

The spirit drenched tete'-a- tete' had been so powerful it had changed deeply rooted agnostic views the woman had held far too long.

In a God inspired moment she had been changed into a born-again believer.

The freedom Delilah felt had bought so much joy to her soul that she had danced all the way down the street.

Etta Mae had spotted her jubilant sister dancing down the sidewalk and had invited her into the car. Etta Mae had rejoiced mightily upon hearing her sister's liberating testimony.

Etta Mae, Tonika, and Dee were all caught up in the Spirit as His presence filled the vehicle. Chains that once had them all bound were instantly broken.

The glorious atmospheric condition that had enveloped that vehicle was one of the highest spiritual levels Tonika had ever experienced. Remorseful feelings had flowed like a river.

Seemingly, the dislike her and Delilah once shared between one another miraculously had dissipated in the course of the afternoon.

Etta Mae's planned route for home had hit a snag due to an informative phone call from Donnie.

She had been asked to drop Delilah off at a hotel downtown where Delilah's estranged husband waited.

Prayerfully, Tonika thought, to a possible love renewal.

Admittedly, she didn't know much about the situation, only what little she had garnered from Etta Mae's limited knowledge.

Her own home drama wasn't far from her mind. The recent discoveries concerning her health, and her marriage was beyond understanding.

"Lord, since you're handing out blessings; don't forget about me! Please don't forget about me!"

It was the prayer she had prayed while in her friend's Spirit saturated vehicle.

Josh had rung her cell phone soon afterwards. The anguish she felt over what led up to their recent separation was waning just a bit.

Through no fault of her own, she had basically become a scorned woman.

Seemingly, overnight she had become a woman rejected in love. She had become very angry.

Her stomach had been in knots dealing with the situation along with the health scare she received through a letter from her doctor.

But now, it seems the Lord had remembered her after all. She had broken out in song.

"I just can't fight this feel-ing; deep inside of me…"

Huh? The two other occupants of the car uttered.

"Teehee… I feel 'ya brothah!" Tonika said in agreement.

"What? You can't fight the feeling of hearing your Boo's voice?" Etta Mae asked.

She said this all in jest as she knew a little background of her friend's troubled marriage.

"Oh, it's nothing. Tonika, the tall statuesque, beauty had responded.

The gray Audi proceeded down the street. Tonika offered another suggestion.

"You know what Etta Mae? Since you're taking Dee to the hotel; why don't you let me out right here?"

Tonika began gathering her purse. She reached for the door handle but paused to hear what Etta Mae had to say.

Oh! So you're going to walk home? Etta Mae responded. Are you alright?"

"I'm fine, if you must know." Tonika shook her head. In fact, I couldn't be better!"

"I guess that phone call really do have you feeling some sort of way." Etta Mae responded.

Dee watched the interaction between the two from the confines of the back seat.

Perhaps fences needed mending in the neighbor's relationship also. Dee thought.

She didn't know much about the Gibbon's marriage, but from what she could see her sister's friend was eager enough to get it started.

I wish her the best of luck. Dee thought. Well, maybe not luck, but perhaps an intervention by way of the Prophet. Dee chuckled.

"No." Tonika commented. "It's just that since we're so close to home, it'd be best you go directly to the hotel from here."

Then she thought to add.

"Besides, walking will give me a chance to think before I reach home."

"I know what you mean." Dee added. "My walk this afternoon sure had a profound effect on me."

"I'll say it did." Etta Mae joined in. "You haven't even lied girlfriend."

The three women had a laughing moment.

"Well, okay then." Etta Mae said to her friend. She reached over and gave Tonika a quick hug.

"We'll connect later. Oh! And I pray you don't meet up with anything not of this world!" Etta Mae chokingly said.

"No chance of my doing that." Tonika laughingly said while exiting the car.

She had met Dee as she proceeded to take her place in the front seat.

Then something unique happened. The two women had stopped and hugged each other.

[1] *"Friendship that flows from the heart cannot be frozen by adversity..."* Dee began.

[2] *"As the water that flows from the spring cannot congeal in winter."* Tonika completed.

Words of James Fenimore Cooper quoted simultaneously by what were once mere acquaintances had now formed a union of kindred spirits.

The women actually hugged. Who knew we both liked the works of James Fenimore Cooper! Tonika thought.

After saying their goodbyes Tonika had struck out at a brisk pace.

"Whew! I've got to slow down."

She breathlessly declared after walking at a physically demanding pace.

"Humph! Apparently, I'm not as agile as I once thought."

The administrative assistant in BARNEY & GREY Law Firm walked at a much slower gait.

It would appear the slower saunter was more therapeutic than she thought as she began actively appreciating the panoramic view of the neighborhood.

Humph! She thought. This certainly rivals the effects of merely driving this route every day.

The topography of bright vibrant colors of flowering bushes and green manicured lawns was giving her a sense of euphoria.

Birds chirped in low hanging branches of majestic trees lining the street.

She chuckled as a bushy-tailed squirrel scurried down a big oak tree simply to pick up one acorn that had fallen from his grasp.

"Sometimes you feel like a nut; sometimes you don't. Huh, little guy?"

His squirrely antics held her gaze for a short while.

"Well, I can tell you this little friend; you're not alone."

She mulled over in her mind what she would say, or what she would do once she reached home.

Tonika reached up to adjust thick heavy locks that held in a ponytail before moving on.

"I can't believe I'm this tired."

She thought of the letter she'd received from her doctor. The news wasn't good.

Tonika made a decision to rest a bit on a park bench she spotted just ahead.

As she reached the bench, a light mist appeared enveloping her in a fog.

That's strange. The tired pedestrian thought to herself.

Its late evening, so why is it so foggy?

Hesitant steps took the skeptical woman further into the eerie mist.

"Oh my!"

Suddenly, the mist parted, only to reveal a startling womanly figure sitting on the bench. Getting closer the wraith's mode of dress was a good indication of the Bible era.

"OMG…ah!" Tonika gasped.

Nothing is off limits to this madness, first Etta Mae's home, the mall, and now here. She thought.

"Oh, now that's just great! I thought this sort of thing only happen with Etta Mae. She's the New Jersey medium; not me!

Tonika paused for a brief moment, but soon accepted the fact of yet another encounter with a supernatural phenomenon was unavoidable.

The fledgling Bible scholar was somewhat confused about the specter's identification.

"Who? No, don't tell me… but you're Ruth, or, or that, that Orpah chick… aren't you?"

But no response was forth coming from the silent figure.

Tonika chose to sit down on the bench. Long dark tresses hung haphazardly obscuring the waif's face from full view. The woman looked to be in her late teens or very early twenties.

A small rip on the sleeve of her white cotton under dress was visibly noticeable. Not to mention, the red overlay tied with a white rope was a bit smudged.

A blue linen scarf that once draped the damsel's head was now grasped in small trembling fingers that lay in her lap.

Tonika was taking the vision all in. Though a bit dusty, small feet were adorned in strappy leather sandals.

It seemed like an eternity before a small whisper of a voice emerged from between quivering lips. The voice was tinged with a hint of sadness.

"They brought me to Him and made me stand before Him. Then they said, "Teacher, this woman was caught in the act of adultery, and the Law of Moses commands us to stone such a woman.

Tonika listened intently. She now knew whose company she was now in; "the woman caught in adultery in John 8.

The woman's story was indeed riveting. Etta Mae had talked at length during their last week's Bible study of the unfortunate damsel.

Oooh! This should be good. She thought. The story is coming straight from the perpetrator's own mouth. Wait 'til my friend hears this.

"Now what do you say? They asked Him." The woman continued.

"But His kind sweet face didn't even look at them; neither did he look at me for that matter."

The baffled Bible novice conducted a mental check of her limited knowledge of Scripture.

"Was your… Uh uhmm!" Tonika hesitantly began to ask. "I mean, was he, your fellow adulterer; was he really in the crowd?"

Tonika framed the question with *a* double finger quote, but received no reply to her intrusive question.

"It was all just a trick."

"A trick?" The flustered bench-mate interjected.

"Come on… help me out here. Who was tricking who… or whom rather?"

But the tawdry tale continued on with no recognition of her bench mate's curiosity.

"It was at one of the busiest times in the city, the Feast of Tabernacle, when those slippery scoundrels tried to catch the 'Teacher' in a vice.

At this point, Tonika thought it pointless trying to get clarification from the young mystic seated next to her on the bench.

She made a valiant effort to appear unfazed by the complexity of it all.

The guilt of not fully listening during Bible study came back to haunt her. She was certain the woman's plight had been explained by her Bible-thumping friend.

"You know what… it sounds like you just need a good listener."

Tonika sat back and folded her arms.

"So that's just what I'll do. Just sit here and listen."

Just wait 'til I tell my friend about this one. She couldn't help but think.

Her decision mattered little to the story teller as she continued on with her tale.

"The law actually required both parties caught in the sin of adultery be executed.

"And that would be like right!" Tonika interjected. "After all, it does take two to tango!"

"T-tango?"

"Yeah, tango…it's when… oh, never mind just continue with your story."

"Well…okay then." *The specter solemnly began her tale once again.*

"If the Teacher had said not to "stone me" it would've looked as though He was flagrantly disregarding the Law.

But it didn't matter to my accusers, because they were only taking part of the law into account.

Rather than giving them His answer, the Teacher just bent down and wrote on the Temple floor with His finger. I know even in your day, everyone is wondering what He was writing.

"Riddle me this." Tonika breaking her declared silence had to ask.

"What exactly did He write? You had to know; you were there."

I can't tell you what was written, because the temple's floor was stone. But, here's the thing… maybe the Teacher was merely, what you call today, 'ghost writing.'

Maybe it was His way of reminding the religious leaders how Moses' law was written on stone tablets by the finger of God on Mt. Sinai.

"Hmmm" Tonika pondered. "You may be right about that one. Hey!"

It suddenly darned on her the woman was surprisingly responding to her questioning.

Perhaps my accusers were reminded that they too were breaking the law themselves by not bringing my guilty accomplice to face the same fate as me.

Then, the Teacher stood and said, "If any one of you is without sin, let him be the first to throw a stone at her."

Tonika dared not interrupt again. There was no need as she was getting far more information than she had first thought.

He knelt once again and began writing. But my accusers, even though they were draped in all their religious and fabric finery, were as naked as they'd ever been, standing before Him.

My accusers own sins I'm sure, were playing out in their own minds.

And slowly, one by one, the 'stones of death' began to drop. And one by one they all turned and went their separate way.

Her bench companion couldn't help but sit quietly in awe with mouth agape.

Tonika could only envision what that must've been like. After a brief pause the saga continued.

Then, when my accusers were no longer there, Jesus spoke to me for the first time. There I was, standing there while He was still kneeling.

And when the Teacher stood up he turned to me. "Where are they? Has no one condemned you?" He asked me.

"No one," I answered. And do you know what?

"What? Tonika answered.

"It was then I called Him "Lord. The waif said.

"Then neither do I condemn you." He told me.

"Neither do I?" Tonika repeated. "That's what Jesus said to you?"

"Here's a thought." She added. "Have you ever wondered why He didn't condemn you? I mean you did do the despicable act didn't you?"

She couldn't help but ask the question. The phenomena pondered on the question before answering.

"I guess maybe," she began, "perhaps for all the nakedness of my sin; He knew the condition of my heart. After all, I had already repented"

"Well... I do know the Lord is "all knowing and He's all seeing." Tonika proudly added. "Now I do know that much." He's omniscient!"

The unkempt red tresses were slowly brushed back from the hidden face revealing glistening hazel green eyes situated in a wistful face.

"To-nika, I believe? Where I was spiritually at that moment in time, the circumstances of my situation was small in comparison to where I once was!"

"It was only after the Lord said those words, "neither do I condemn you," that I knew He was the Messiah I'd heard about as a little girl."

"So, let me get this straight," Tonika began. "For starters, you were caught in sin, and you were about to die. Then unbeknownst to you or your accusers Jesus saved you?"

She thought for a minute before adding.

"Humph! I can see why you would become a believer."

A true genuine camaraderie was beginning to form between the former stalemates.

"That's exactly what I'm saying."

"And it couldn't have been because you somehow knew "only God can forgive sin? Now am I right?"

"Yes… yes you are correct."

She then turned giving Tonika her full attention.

"And I perceive you're also a godly woman, "but… yet your life is in direct parallel to mine in some ways."

The surprising revelation of her tumultuous life's current situation caused an immediate reaction.

Tonika jumped up and threw up both her hands.

""Oh, can I just put a praise on that? Yes, Lord!"

The entity now had the bereft bench mate's full attention. Tonika returned to her seat.

"And I'm not even gonna' ask; how do you know that?"

Giving the deceptive circumstances she currently faced Tonika was beyond being shocked.

"It's not surprising to me you would know what I'm going through at home… and even in my health."

"It is true. I am privy to your information. And you wouldn't be alone." The divulger of secrets added. *"That's just Jezebel's M-O; disrupting marriages, churches, or any other God sanctioned union."*

"Then to know all this, you must be a part of those 'witnesses in the clouds' my best friend keep telling me about."

"The 'great cloud of witnesses' you mean?"

"Yes, those guys!" Tonika said, throwing her head back.

"Let's see... Noah should be in there, you know the man in the ark, Abraham... and let's see Jacob, etcetera, etcetera, in that cloud."

"If you're referring to the patriarchs of old who died in faith... then yes, you're correct they're all a part of that cloud."

"And you know this because..."

The specter curiously inquired of Tonika.

"Oh! It's just that it's what the Bible says in Hebrew chapter eleven. Tonika said. "I'm surprised you didn't know that."

The woman simply chuckled.

"Well... can I also tell you, my friend Etta Mae Smith and me had some unexpected visitor's all day today, beginning with-

"Eve, Mrs. Potiphar and that woman, Jezebel! Yes, I saw them all.

"Oh, don't get me started on those ladies!" Tonika said. "How're they in the cloud?"

"Who says they're in the cloud?" Then the woman thought to add. *"And besides, it's not for me to determine who makes up the witness list."*

A moment passed as the two sat in deep thought before the waif spoke once again.

"Are you aware there's a spirit realm all around you?"

"Yes Lord! Who don't know it?" Tonika responded. "One can't help but know when you have mediums, psychics, and those necromancers talking to spirits all the time!"

"It would seem portals have been opened to the spirit realm and the natural realm."

"I just don't know what this world is coming to!" Tonika added. "Is it a good thing, or is it a bad thing?"

"Search your scripture then ask yourself was it meant for one to find a happy medium between the two worlds?"

"Hmmmm! You may have a point there. Etta Mae and I certainly have a job to do."

Etta Mae's home was certainly one of comfort. One could find solace there. Tonika made it a point to converse or visit with her friend at least once a day.

One usually can't be in the same company with Mrs. Smith without ending up in an impromptu Bible study.

Daily, Etta Mae, her best friend could often be found thumping pages of her Bible.

This would often result to her correlating today's hot topics with likewise biblical happenings.

Little had she known just how invasive the 'spirit realm' would invade her 'here and now.'

Perhaps this is all the 'Twilight Zone.' She thought.

She somehow expected Rod Sterling to suddenly appear out of nowhere and yell; "Psych!"

The invasive words the woman next spoke cut sharply into Tonika's engaging thoughts.

"And you weren't alone in the visitation of that woman Jezebel, because, I'm sorry to say, your husband, Josh also fell under her spell."

"Oh, that hussy!" Tonika shouted. "I should've wiped that darn smirk off her face when I had a chance!"

The enormity of it all had Tonika totally flabbergasted.

Her desperate need to get home resurfaced once again.

"But, enough about that! I'm on my way home now. My husband is there… but the sad thing is I don't know what to expect when I get there."

The woman looked hard and long at the assignment seated next to her before she spoke.

"I can tell you this, Tonika. Josh won't be the same man as when you last saw him."

A look of astonishment came over Tonika's countenance.

"He won't; how…?" She asked the adulterous woman. "H-how do you know? On second thought, don't answer that."

The waif emitted a soft chuckle before she went on to add.

"In fact, he has something important to tell you once you get there."

Tonika grabbed at her chest, and inhaled a deep breath of air.

"What… that he wants a divorce?"

"I'm afraid the answer to that question," the woman stated, *"will greatly depend on where your heart lie.*

And just how, may I ask, does it all depend on me?"

Tonika pondered the woman's words. Was it I who committed adultery?

Knowing what must've been going through her subject's mind, the woman said to the despondent bench mate.

"You... supposedly have accepted Jesus Christ as your Lord and Savior; have you not?"

A silent moment passed before Tonika responded.

"Yes, yes I have!" Tonika almost shouted. "And I know exactly where you're going with this."

"Then you know He who showed me grace and praise God mercy in my deadly dilemma His Spirit now lives in you."

"Who're you telling? I know I have the Holy Spirit. Tonika flippantly said.

"Then listen with your heart to what He is saying and I promise you... you'll be just fine."

"I was listening for the Holy Spirit just as I was walking, but then...

"But then my friend, you encountered me."

The woman rose from her seat and for the first time looked earnestly at her bench mate.

"Yes, I feel as if I can now call you friend"

Tonika nodded her head in total agreement, ready to receive what wisdom and knowledge she was sure was coming forth.

The phantom woman went on to explain how God saw marriage.

"And yes... adultery truly is a major sin. For one thing, it's a sin against God because it makes a mockery of something He has ordained.

But, rest assured, my God and your God is bigger than the infidelity committed in your marriage.

It is only you mortals who believe that sort of thing to be virtually impossible to be forgiven."

The woman's remarks didn't set too well with the scorned housewife. She reminded the woman of the position she herself was caught in.

"You're the one to talk! You were caught in the very act yourself!"

"True, true, but 'grace and mercy' was standing there to forgive me. And I accepted His forgiveness."

The waif added.

"And the only thing He requested from me was that I "go, and sin no more."

"Well…did you?"

"Are you serious? I would be such a fool to return to a life so degrading!"

The surprising outburst startled Tonika to no end.

"Oh my… I certainly struck a nerve on that one."

"There's just no way I would've dishonored the greatest gift ever given to me!"

"You know what?" Tonika finally offered up.

"I can see you as having reached a point of "being sick and tired of being sick and tired."

The statement was met with a look of confusion.

"What I mean is… your life was not prospering you one bit, girlfriend." Tonika stated with liberty.

"Come to think of it… we're never told anything about your life before your encounter with Jesus."

"And just w*hy would it have mattered anyway?*"

"It doesn't matter actually. But were you set up, or!" Tonika added. "Did you go willingly into the man's bed?"

The specter raised a defiant hand, but decidedly allowed it fall once again to her side.

"But I," Tonika poked her own chest with her finger. "I would like to think it was all out of your control."

"As you can attest today, I want you to see the face of your husband instead of my face in that situation."

The woman's candid response floored her bench mate.

"I don't know about back then, but women today are a gamut of emotions." Tonika said.

"Sometimes we even mask our feelings just to keep everyone out. All because we are terrified of being hurt."

At first there was no response to the thoughtful statement. Then the adulterous woman added her input.

"You ask the question; was I guilty or was I falsely accused? Once again, search the scripture. My Lord said to me; "Go and sin no more."

Tonika's eyes widened with full understanding.

At that moment the mysterious fog reappeared and the phenomenon rose up and began to walk away.

The betrayed wife stood watching in silence, fully realizing the adulterous woman's sin was paid on the Cross a few days later after meeting the Lord.

"Good bye…"

Tonika waved.

The solemn apparition turned and offered one last bit of information.

"Thanks for listening. And by the way, that blood situation you're concerned about; well… it was misdiagnosed. You're fine… my friend."

And with those parting words she was gone. A full moment passed before the vastness of it all finally registered.

"Oh praise God! Thank you Jesus!" Tonika shouted in reckless abandonment.

Suddenly, a vision of Dee dancing bare feet down the street rejoicing came to the forefront.

"Now I know the feeling Ms. Whitman!" Tonika shouted aloud. "Okay girlfriend, it's time to go home."

After a distance as Tonika rounded the bend, she could see into her friend's back yard.

Donnie was having an in-depth conversation with little McKenzie over the fence.

As she got closer to home Tonika heard Mrs. Reid call out to Mckenzie.

Out of nowhere, the little 'tumbling tumble weed' did an impressive back flip.

"Oooh! You go Mac!" Tonika said amused at the little imp's antics.

God only knows what brought that on. The neighbor thought as she prepared to turn in to her home.

Josh stood at the window and was about to take his seat once again.

But he suddenly did a double take. A broad smile broke across the relieved husband's face. The most beautiful woman he had ever seen was briskly walking up the sidewalk.

Tonika Gibbons, his wife had finally come home.

CHAPTER

And when Saul inquired of the Lord, the Lord did not answer him, either by dreams, or by Urim, or by prophets. ⁷Then Saul said to his servants, "Seek out for me a woman who is a medium, that I may go to her and inquire of her." And his servants said to him, "Behold, there is a medium at En-dor."
1 Samuel 28:6-7

A few days later, Donnie is on the golf course as usual and Etta Mae is doing what she does best; studying the Word.

Delilah had returned for her belongings on last evening. She had informed her sister earlier she and Damien were talking things out and plan to return home soon.

Etta Mae rose from the dining table and went into the spotless kitchen to refresh her coffee.

As she returned to the dining room she heard a light knock on the door.

"It's open!" She yelled fully knowing who's on the other side of the door.

"Hey Toni. You're out awfully early this morning."

Tonika walked into the dining room and plopped down. Etta Mae placed the cup of coffee she was about to sip on a coaster.

"Hey tootsie; what're you up to this fine morning?"

The question was met with a whimsical smirk and wave of a hand.

"Oh, I'd say… right about 5'7, 130 pounds!"

Tonika ended up laughing at her own pun.

"Oh! Aren't we funny?"

Etta Mae couldn't keep the frustrations of this week from showing.

"Awww! Ms. Smith, I'm just kidding with 'ya!"

Tonika thought perhaps she could lighten the mood with a little jab.

"Besides, I knew old 'nine iron' was on the golf course as usual, so, I just came over to tell you something."

She had come over for a little girl-chat. Tonika was eager to discuss the recent happenings of sort, but most importantly she wanted to share the encounter she had with the 'adulterous woman.'

She would have come over sooner, but she knew certain episodes in her best friend's life warranted her own undivided attention.

Delilah, Etta Mae's middle sister and husband had certainly brought drama to what was once a docile and peaceful household.

Etta Mae inserted her digit finger into her Bible before closing it.

She inhaled deeply then slowly released the air and locked onto her friend's eyes.

"You're right… Donnie is on the green, but as you can well see I'm in good company right now… me and the Word."

She held up the book and waved it back and forth.

But Tonika's light-hearted banter continued in spite of her friend's solemn demeanor.

She refused to accept the discernible slight.

"You know what girlfriend; I was just in my Word this morning!"

Finding what she had just heard unfathomable, Etta Mae's finger slipped from between the pages while focusing intently on her house guest.

"Oh, you don't say." She said. "Now I'm definitely impressed!"

Her eyes moved from the confrontational stare back to the closed Bible.

"As well as you should be!"

Tonika chuckled at her efforts to evoke a more receptive atmosphere.

"Oh, alright now girl. Now you know you crazy. Go pour yourself a cup of brew."

This time it was the homeowner's time to chuckle.

"I can't be annoyed around you."

Tonika went into the kitchen and returned with piping hot coffee. She sat down at the table.

"You know still the question remains though."

Tonika took a sip of the hot beverage and reacted with an inquisitive facial expression.

"Ooh! That's hot! And just what question would that be?"

Etta Mae pushed the container of sugar and creamer towards her before answering.

"Did you fully understand what it was you read?"

Tonika was undoubtedly elated the atmosphere was finally changing from being strained, but was somewhat puzzled about the question.

"I think it was..." she began hesitantly, then saying more assuredly.

"It was Two Kings! Yes, yes, that was it!"

Her elation however was short lived.

"But, as far as my understanding it. Goes...we-ll."

Etta Mae's eyes widened at the mere mispronunciation of the biblical scripture.

"Correct me if I'm wrong Bible scholar, but I think you mean Second Kings!"

Tonika covered her mouth to hide a sheepish grin.

"Sorry, forgive my 'Trump' moment. Of course I meant second."

She hadn't really read the passage, but knew the talk of scripture was one way to electrify her friend's mood.

True, she did love the scriptures, but there was no way, she thought, she would ever be on the level of her Bible-thumping neighbor.

"It's good to hear you're searching."

Etta Mae knew her neighbor well enough to know she may've opened the Bible out of sheer whim.

"What is it you want to know? Tonika flippantly asked. "I can't think of a better way to start the morning."

A moment of truth overcomes Tonika and she decides to share the truth with her written Word tutor.

"Aww, sistah-girl, the truth is… well, to be perfectly honest." she stuttered. "I-I opened my Bible this morning… but child wouldn't you know it! I somehow got distracted!"

The 'Patty Greenhorn's remark was met with quaint skepticism.

But the stuttering fledgling was given the benefit of the doubt.

"Honey that was nothing but the 'enemy!'

"Huh? What?" Tonika asked amazed.

"What I mean is Satan don't want people of God to know the truth—

"You trying to say Satan stopped me from my quest to read my Word this morning?"

Tonika asked while thinking on her faith nemesis.

"You got a better explanation?" Etta Mae countered.

The question was met with an emphatic declaration.

"Well, if you call my son's constantly yelling; "Mom-mie, where is; or Mom-mie, I can't find my— Satan then… yes!"

Still feeling a tad perturbed Tonika went on to declare.

"To put it bluntly, I woke up this morning thinking; "Lord, why's my life so… so; how can I say this? So… blah?"

The self-pity moment was not wasted on the unconvinced neighbor who in turn responded with a gesture of playing an imaginary violin.

"Da, da dee, da da dee… woe is me. Poor little ole me…"

"Ouch! Can I say your attitude stinks this morning?"

But the onslaught had only begun.

"Well quit it with the woe-is-me pity-party then, Missy!" Etta Mae went on to add. "I don't have time for it this morning!"

"Ouch again!"

"Well, what you're going through is called pride and God's not pleased with it… In fact, He hates it!"

"What ant got into your drawers this morning?" Tonika wanted to know. "I didn't mean anything by what I said."

Etta Mae offered no answer.

"I'm sorry, but I can't even express how I feel before you go off———

"Girl…" Etta Mae countered. "I'm so sorry, but you just happened to catch me at a bad time."

A pang of remorse shot through Tonika's spirit. She exhaled and picked up a discarded magazine.

Compared to her usual jovial demeanor her friend's unfamiliar attitude this morning is somewhat unnerving.

Tonika couldn't remember if she'd ever witnessed her 'Rock of Gilbraltar' in such a state of despair in their twenty year friendship.

"Oh, it's just that I've never known you to be so critical." Tomika begins rising from the seat.

"So if you'll excuse me, I'll just take my leave… sorry I bothered you."

A restraining hand stopped her in mid stride.

"Aw, girl, just sit down." Etta Mae directed.

Her friend's eye opening remark had brought the homeowner's acute awareness of just how disgruntled her demeanor appeared.

"For some reason I'm just not myself this morning" The Bible-thumper offered. "I guess I'm still worried and concerned about my sister and her situation."

"Oh, honey, they're alright. Tomika said.

"I'm truly hoping they are." The concerned sister stated. "She certainly seemed to be when she called from the hotel suite last night."

"Oh, that's nice. I saw her earlier when she came to pick up her suitcase.

"It looks like progress has been made." Etta Mae said.

"Well, I for one am glad. You do know me and Dee became friends, don't you?"

Etta Mae answered the question with a smirk and an eye roll.

"Um humm… so it would seem."

"Yeah, when we got out of your car Dee began reciting James Fenimore Cooper."

"Who knew you two were so versed in the man's work?"

"Now about that." Tonika said. I think it's a form of art myself. Even if there are a few chinks here and there."

Tonika thought to ask her friend just how adept she was in literature.

"So… tell me this missy. Have you read the Dearslayer?"

"No. And I'm not sorry to say that I haven't." Etta Mae pointedly said. "And if you think I'm going to; think again. Besides my vote is on reading God's Word."

"Ya da, ya da, ya da." Tonika added, while deciding to antagonize her friend a little further.

"Now that I do know, but surely you've read *the Last of the Mohicans*."

The expected rise she was getting out of her now perturbed friend caused the grinning antagonist to double over in laughter.

"Would you please?" Etta Mae shouted. "Enough with the literary lessons!"

"Okay… but I have to ask why you're still worried about your sister's life when it looks like things were workin—"

"Why? I'll tell you why," Etta Mae defiantly said. "Because looks can be somewhat deceiving! That's why."

"Well… you know she did leave with her man in tow so…".

"Plus, the two appeared to be on good terms from where I was sitting."

"And from where I'm sit-ting," Etta Mae emphatically stated, "a lot of questions still need answering. At least for me; that is."

Tonika met the counter active comment with a simple shrug and got up to peer out the window.

"What can you say? It could be the 'man in white' made a big change in your sister's outlook on life. What do you think?"

"I think…" Etta Mae began. "If you must know; 'that man in white' made a change in more lives than my sister's."

Tonika knew all too well what the man of mystery appearance had accomplished. Her friend's next remark served as a reminder.

"Don't forget your man Josh was also privy to all his wisdom. Remember?"

Tonika was glad her back was turned as she winced from the memory of her recent marriage drama.

"Will wonders never cease? Yes… I remember!" She exclaimed.

She suddenly began pushing the nearly empty cup back and forth between nervous hands.

"Humph… child, it's still a work in progress."

The scenery outside the window now had her full attention.

Etta Mae grasped her friend's hands and held them firmly still.

The simple gesture was enough to snap the daydreamer out of her trance.

"Thanks girl! My mind wandered there a bit."

A fit of laughter engulfed them both.

"Girrl... You're welcome." Etta Mae was able to say between guffaws while holding her stomach.

After a bit, unaccustomed silence fell among the two as they were each locked in different states of lethargy.

The neighbor's right foot kept up a nervous tapping beneath the table.

Finally, Etta Mae broke the silence with a request.

"Tell me more about your close up with the "adulterous woman."

"I actually liked her." Tonika stated.

"You what?"

"I actually liked her because I think she was just a victim of her circumstances."

Seeing the disbelief on her friend's face she continued with her explanation.

"Well, you couldn't help but feel sorry for the woman."

"True, true." Etta Mae said thoughtfully before changing the subject. Oh, I didn't tell you. I ran into Sis-tah Edna a few days ago."

"Old Motor Mouth Eddie Brown? I thought Stephanie was bad, but that woman will talk your head off. And don't forget her husband Roscoe is a talker too."

"That's strange." Etta Mae said. "I'm shocked the man can get a word in edge-wise!

"Well, don't be! Eddie's always running off at the mouth, but her other half takes up her slack so..."

"A-nd not to mention," Tonika added, "when it comes to the Word, girl-friend, you have some strong competition."

"And girlfriend..." Etta Mae countered. "I have you know Edna Brown talks more than the Word! Don't let her get a hold your story."

"Who're you telling? The woman's a virtual walking newspaper!" Laughter fills the kitchen once again.

Etta Mae was about to place the morning dishes in the sink when she notices the jacket cover of the cd *Ghost*, lying on the kitchen counter. She had watched it last night while preparing supper. The recent supernatural events came to the fore front of her mind, causing her feel as if she could solely identify with Whoopi's character, Oda Mae Brown. Picking up the CD cover, and turning to Tonika Etta Mae said to her neighbor.

"Now just humor me a moment Toni. Okay?"

The seriousness in her friend's voice prompted Tonika to say.

"Okay… what's on your mind girlfriend?"

"Just that… now I could be wrong, but I believe we have what Oda Mae Brown had."

"Are you serious?" A befuddled Tonika sat listening with full attention.

"Girl! Don't you get it?" Etta Mae asked. "Y-You remember' the woman could see spirits!"

"Oh yeah, you're right. All the lost souls were joggling to come through."

Acute awareness replaces the perplexed expression on the face.

"You know what? You're right Etta. Now I remember that scene." Tonika has a little laugh before continuing.

"Ha! Oda Mae was hilarious! Whoopi played that part!"

Etta Mae's revelation had come as no shock to Tonika.

"Etta Mae!!" Tonika suddenly shouted with a surprising look on her face.

"What?" Etta Mae answered. "What's wrong?"

"Does that mean… w-we're mediums too!" Tonika exclaimed.

"Ooo! You know, you may be right Sistah-Girl!"

The temperature in the room appeared to have dropped a degree or two. The two women shivered.

"It seems the spirit world has found a 'happy medium;' no-correction; two- two happy mediums between their world and ours.

The two women found the play on words quite amusing.

"I get it; hap-py medium!" Tonika laughed aloud.

"You're not Etta Mae Smith! You're now Oda Mae Brown! Ha,ha,ha!

Etta Mae's face lit up with the realization of it all. "Hey... yea! You're right." She said. "You'd think one of us was the 'witch of Endor,' or the Isle of Palms Medium or something."

"Us...you a-and me?" Tonika shouted gleefully. Y-asss honey! Oh, but there's just one thing."

"And what might that be?"

"I'm no witch."

"So you say.' Then Etta Mae added. "Your mission then, "'should you choose to accept it is 1 Samuel 28. Read it!"

"Huh? W-What? Tonika asked.

The Bible novice knew more studying was needed on her part in order to compete with her in tensed Bible knowledge friend.

"That's where you'll learn about the 'witch of En Dor,' girlfriend." Etta Mae stated.

Tonika took the liberty of retrieving an oatmeal cookie from her friend's supposedly hidden stash.

"You know what Etta—

After taking a bite she turned to see a look of astonishment on the homeowner's face.

"Oh, I'm sorry... you thought me and Donnie didn't know where your secret stash were hidden?"

"Well apparently they're no longer a secret."

Etta Mae jokingly added before getting up to retrieve her favorite desert for herself.

"But what was your question?"

"Oh, do you think that's what's going on with all this medium crap on television these days?"

"Huh? What're you going on about girl?"

"It's just that I know you watch television; even after all your Bible studying."

Tonika returned to her seat. "So I know you've seen that blond wire-haired medium."

The Bible-thumper shook her head in confirmation.

"Yes, it's a popular show. And more and more so called mediums are popping up every day!"

"You're right." Tonika acknowledged.

"And I've even seen that young man in Hollywood too, doing readings for the stars. You've seen that show too; haven't you?"

"Yes, and now it seems there's even a young girl following the same path." Etta Mae added.

"Say Etta Mae" Tonika asked in amusement. "Since we seem to have the 'gift', do you suppose we're…

"Uh, hel-lo-o… Newsflash! I'm not Saul; so, no spirits have I called. So you can stop right there."

"But Etta, even Jesus showed up in a room after His resurrection, and the disciples hadn't called him either!"

"And your point!"

"Just that—

"I guess it's a blessing you at least know about Jesus' visit."

It soon became evident to Etta Mae since Tonika hadn't known the scripture of 1 Samuel 28 it was obvious she was more in tune with the New Testament.

It could be her belief like some, was that the Old Testament no longer mattered, and that we only live by the New Testament.

If that was the case then one would be hard pressed to understand the New Testament without knowing the Old Testament.

"You know girl-friend, the Old Testament is the New Testament concealed.

Whereas the New Testament is the Old Testament revealed."

Tonika sat in silence. Her friend had opened her understandings to many Bible scriptures.

But the New Testament seemed to speak more directly to her psyche.

Perhaps that equated to her knowing the 'adulteress woman's saga.

"Etta Mae! How 'bout this?" Tonika excitedly said. "It could be there's a new thing happening and your home may be deemed the new 'Upper Room!"

"You trippin!"

"Think about it girl."

"I'm not even going to honor that with a decent response. You're cuckoo!"

"How can you not think that after what's been happening lately?" Tonika replied.

Even she was amazed she'd hit on an obvious revelation.

"Okay then... riddle me this; first of all, in whose home did our girl 'Eve' pop into? Huh?"

"And then, even later, according to your own husband, Adam came looking for her? Probably the same way he looked for her when she was talking to that dang snake!"

A look of awareness settled over Etta Mae's countenance as she couldn't help but ponder the fact Tonika was making. She had to admit her friend was certainly on to something.

But at the moment a sudden need to visit the restroom afforded the befuddled housewife a welcoming escape.

"Humph! Chile, that coffee is running right through me."

She was already running from the room when she yelled.

"You have to excuse me for a second. I have to make a run!"

Etta Mae made a hasty retreat.

Left to sort through her thoughts Tonika picked up the discarded magazine she was reading earlier.

She lazily flipped through the pages when she is startled by a sudden movement out of the corner of her eye.

Unbeknownst to Tonika, Etta Mae harbored that very same thought.

"Ex-scuzze me for a sec. I'll be right back!"

Etta Mae rose from her chair and scurried off to the restroom.

The bereft young neighbor was left to sort through her own bewildered feelings on the matter.

As a distraction from it all Tonika began flipping through the magazine pages once again.

The bi-racial middle aged woman of Black/German descent had become engrossed in an article when a sudden movement out of the corner of her eye caused the magazine to go flying through the air.

There, standing silently in the center of her friend's kitchen stood a figure of a woman cloaked in darkness.

"Whoa!" She jumped. "Oh, my God!"

Tonika's heart skipped a hurried beat. The frightened human took on a sudden intake of breath.

"Who're you an-and wh-what're you doing here?"

Tonika looked long and hard at the materialized intruder. Then suddenly realization hit,

"Ooh no!" Tonika gasped. "I-I know who you are!"

The mystical figure remained silent.

The terrified human bolted from her chair and began backing away, preparing to run all while once again taking in the appearance of the specter.

The visible incorporeal spirit was something to behold. It was clothed in a black hooded full circle velvet cloak. The foreboding garment obscured the specter's facial features.

Even though a hook and loop mechanism front closure was visible, a slip of red muslin material peaked from beneath the slight opening of the dark cloak.

Her neighbor's home had once again become enshrouded with supernatural occurrences. The pungent smell of smoke permeating the room was a huge indication of of time spent stirring a cauldron.

"Y-You're that-that wi-witch! You're the Witch of En Dor!"

The cloaked figure remained motionless and silent, neither acknowledging, nor denying the human's startling revelation.

Tonika was still able to screech out a frantic call to her friend even in her state of fear and panic.

"E-Etta! Etta Mae! Gir-rl, you-you really need to get in here. An-and I mean fast!"

A door slammed down the hallway. Soon footsteps could be heard running.

"Chile! What're you going on about?" Etta Mae stumbled into the room.

"Oh! Oh my! Where did that come from? Where's my oil? I need my oil!"

The startled homeowner breathed deeply while holding her chest. Notwithstanding, even though she had somehow become accustomed to impromptu visitations by disembodied spirits, this one may invoke the use of a bit of spiritual warfare.

"Gir-rrl, what was that you were saying earlier?"

She reached over to take her friend's hand as they both stood trembling.

"It's the witch." Tonika informed her terrified cohort.

"S-She told you who she was?"

"No!" But just look at her or it! It couldn't be anything else."

"Ummph! Do you smell that?"

"It does smell like something from a forest fire."

"Oo-oh! Oh, no!"

"What; what're you thinking girl?

"Or-or something from Hell!

The two humans shrieked.

Oh, the blood of Jesus! The blood of Jesus!"

The sight of this apparition had more of a fearful effect on the two than any previous apparitions.

Not even the sight of the woman Jezebel had invoked such fright.

The two women were most fearful of possibly being on the other end of a cast spell.

Finally, the figure moved and addressed the frightened women.

The gravelly hoarse voice was nothing like either had ever heard before.

"Why was I summoned?" The figure asked.

Tonika and Etta Mae looked questionably at each other.

"N-No one summoned you." Tonika answered.

"You obviously have us confused with King Saul."

Giving the circumstances, Etta Mae was shocked at the boldness her friend was exhibiting.

Now that dialogue had been established she too found her voice. So she brazenly said to the entity.

"I know your story, but I don't believe I know your name."

"My name is not important, but you were correct in assuming my identity."

"Ooh, that's good to hear." Etta Mae said under her breath.

"I am the witch of En Dor. I was well known throughout my region, but as you know never once was my name mentioned. I preferred it that way."

"I guess you did." Etta Mae said. "After all you were incognito, so…"

"What do you mean she was in-cog-ni—

"Incognito! I simply meant the witch and others like her were in hiding.

The king had banished all witches and mediums from the land. So our pop-in-guest here didn't want to be found."

"I wonder why the king did that." Tonika said. "Did he know something we don't know?"

"Ah yeah! He knew Leviticus 19!" The Bible-thumper proudly said.

"And the word goes on to say "rebellion is like the sin of divination…""

"Sounds about right to me. Maybe Saul thought he was doing God a favor by getting rid of all those diviners."

"It's a possibility." Etta Mae agreed.

"So, Etta, let me ask you this."

"What is it now Tonika?"

"Why are psychics, mediums and-and what's the other one?"

"Necromancers." Etta Mae offered.

"Yeah, those ne-cros; why is what they do considered sinful?"

"For the simple fact God is the all knowing One, and no one knows what's after death, but God!"

"Oh, yeah." Tonika flagrantly said. "It's beyond me why anyone would want to talk to the dead anyway."

The figure listened intently from under the dark cloak.

"Or-rr!" Etta Mae interjected. "Perhaps Saul just wanted to rid the country of "familiar spirits.' You know all those demons, I mean."

"The text reads the Lord had stopped talking to Saul due to his rebellion of God's word.

Saul and his son Jonathan were about to go to war. But he was afraid and wanted to know the outcome."

"Oka-ay, okay. Then what does that have to do with our girl here?"

Tonika directed her question to her friend who responded by saying.

"Don't you get it, dunce…we, as the creation are not suppose to know what's to happen from one minute to the next. Or what the dead is doing for that matter.

Only the 'the Creator' Himself is privy to that knowledge. Once again, God is the 'all knowing One;' not you, not me, or that standing in my kitchen! And anyone who think otherwise is a bald-faced liar!"

Tonika not meaning for her cohort to become so riled up by the innocent question responded with a sarcastic reply.

"And it's too bad they can't ask you. 'Miss Know Everything.' Geez!"

The fact the two women were so caught up in their reasoning's the lone figure chose to intervene.

"Since I was there, please allow me to answer some of your questions."

The two were taken aback by the entity's directness.

"Oh, by all means." Etta Mae responded. But before she could respond, Tonika had something to say.

"I can see how you would be called a witch giving your attire. And we haven't even seen your face so—

"Perhaps this will help."

What happened next shocked the two onlookers beyond belief. They watched as two small alabaster hands abruptly appeared from beneath the long sleeves of the dark cloak.

The two ladies watched as the hands reached up and slid the hood of the cloak back from the obscured face.

"Ooh my!" Etta Mae exclaimed.

"Dayum!" Tonika let slip. "I-I mean darn!"

Once the hood was removed they could see ringlets of black charcoal tresses framing an oval face. A rogue strand of hair hanging callously concealing one of the ice blue eyes set deeply under contoured brows.

A finely chiseled nose cast a distinctive shadow over thin parted lips tinted with a hint of color. Those same lips perhaps hadn't smiled for centuries.

To put it bluntly, the phantom figure was no where the hideous troll the two had vividly imagined. In fact, she was totally the opposite.

And as for her attire, even though a hook and loop mechanism front closure was visible on the dark cloak. A slip of red woolen material peaked from beneath the slight opening.

The witch went on to unhook the mechanism and allowed the outer garment to fall fully to the floor.

She wore a long white tunic undergarment. The sleeves of the white tunic reached to delicate elbows. The whole garment was over layered with a large red piece of rough, heavy woolen material cast over her left shoulder.

Well-worn cowhide leather sandals were strapped to strong legs supporting a tall lithe body.

"Okay… now that does help."

Tonika was the first to say. She looked to Etta Mae for agreement.

"Now, that does put things into better prospective. So, as you were saying…"

"What I was saying was…no doubt, in your world today, witches are thought of as evil and frightening. But, I have you two know, although I was thought to be a witch, I did not practice the dark rituals and tricks as you've imagined."

"Lies you tell! "A wit—

"Tonika! Girl, don't forget who, or what we're dealing with here. Girrrl….don't get it twisted; we might end up as two frogs sitting on log if you don't watch it."

The callous interruption hadn't phased the specter the least bit.

"I simply indulged in the art of talking with the dead. I believe you call us mediums today."

"And you would be correct."

"I guess what I'm trying to say is; I'm not evil."

Tonika's eyes rolled in their sockets.

"And just whose word do we have on that?"

The specter chose to go on with her storytelling in lieu of answering the human's insoluble question.

"Even though the troubled king deceived me, I merely did what I was asked. I could've been stoned."

"He deceived you?"

"Yes, Tonika, Saul was in disguise so she didn't know it was him."

"But, a wit— I mean a medium is supposed to already know these things. You get me?"

The home owner twisted uneasily in her chair. She was hoping to find a way to keep her friend from making the specter angry.

"So just what does that tell you? Either I wasn't on my game, or—

"Or that 'familiar spirit' that possessed you left you hanging if you know what I mean."

Silence fell in the room as the specter mulled over what Etta Mae had spoken.

"You may be correct, because even I was surprised when I first saw the spirit of a man rising up.

And I was the only one to see the old man. Then the king asked me what he looked like and what the specter was wearing.

The king was the one who said it was the prophet Samuel.

That's when I knew the man making the request was actually Saul. I was frightened for my very life! But he promised me he wouldn't kill me. It turns out he was true to his word."

"Do you mean to say you trusted your very life to a man you hadn't seen before?" Tonika interjected. "Better you than me, sister."

"No, sister; let me help you. From my study of the scripture, to me she was not an evil person, because after Saul fainted from fasting she rescued the man."

The disembodied guest looked long and hard at the two humans.

One, she thought, appear to know quite a bit about my life saga. Perhaps this Etta Mae is right. After all I was human once too. Even I once possessed natural compassion.

"Now from where I'm sitting I have to say that took compassion. And I also read where you even let the man's servants lay him on your bed!"

"Umph! Chile, again I say better you than me! I don't like other people's butts on my bed. Eeww!!"

A sharp look of rebuttal from Etta Mae cut her friend's rambling short.

"Then… to top it all off, you even made the man a meal."

"You are right in all you have spoken. Saul got the answer he was searching for. He and his men ate; and they ate well. I even made unleavened bread!"

"You see! Etta Mae exclaimed. Unleavened bread! Surely you know what that means!"

"It means when I was me I could be empathetic. But, sadly the me in me had become a pawn to the 'lord of the Netherworld' all due to my unsavory practices.

Even Tonika felt a pang of empathy for the specter's plight.

"And I heard you even slaughtered your only fatted calf. Now that had to take some doing."

"Yes, the calf was my last source of sustenance, but, even still my life was spared. If only I could say that about my soul."

"That's too bad." Etta Mae said. "It's bad because one wonders what you may've become if only you had repented. If only you had cried out to the Lord. It's unfortunate how you remained a pawn of Satan."

Tonika sat in deep thought listening to the intense discussion around her.

"And it's also sad because unlike the girl in Acts 16 was delivered from a familiar spirit; no one was there to deliver you."

"Ooh! Go on now sister. I'm scared of you!"

Etta Mae was shocked at her friend's surprising wisdom. It was it seems just as she had thought.

The scripture novice was more adept in the writings of the New Testament than she was of the Old Testament.

"Be that as it may; "The die is cast.""

"Yes… That event has happened. Your decision was made. And no, it cannot be changed."

The look of confusion from Tonika's face was erased by Etta Mae's remark.

"Ooh… I remember now. She was speaking Latin!

"Duh!"

As the two humans reveled in their moment the specter reached down and retrieved her cloak from the floor.

"We all have our crosses to bear. And no, I didn't worship the God of Israel, but nonetheless, He used me to convey a clear message to the king."

The witch exhaled a long breath before she spoke again.

"I had to tell the unfortunate man what I was told by the prophet Samuel; "tomorrow the Philistines would surely win the battle."

But, what had to be most heartbreaking was that not only Saul, but also his son would lose their lives.

"Umph! My, my, my."

Etta Mae pondered the witch's words.

Now with her cloak securely fastened, the witch once again pulled the hood over her tousled mane.

Her surprisingly revealed face was once again cloaked in darkness. But before vanishing into thin air she had one last thing to say to the humans before her departure.

"Ladies, it seems your God can use even a person dedicated to Satan to do His will. Therefore, your world really needs to awaken to his Sovereignty and submit wholeheartedly to His voice before it's too late."

And with that bit of advice, the specter vanished as quickly and as silently as she had appeared.

One could hear a strand of hair fall to the floor in the deafening silence. The two women sat for awhile in awe of what had just been said.

"Will wonders never cease." Tonika said finally breaking the silence. "The word was just preached to us by a witch."

CHAPTER
Seven

*Now about spiritual gifts, brothers,
I do not want you to be ignorant.
1 Corinthians 12:1 NIV*

Despite the distraction of a whining toddler vowing for her attention, the petite dark haired mother of two pushed her cart through the doors of the Beltway Supermarket.

The youngster's irritable nature was probably due to a back molar forcibly making its way up in his lower jaw.

While absent-mindedly wheeling her empty grocery cart down the organic vegetable aisle, Amanda Culvers stopped dead in her tracks.

She was suddenly being overtaken by an unshakable feeling of sadness. Amanda knew that feeling all too well.

These were parasitic feelings belonging to someone in her near vicinity. Amanda is what is known as an Empath.

Even she was finding it hard to understand her natural intuition about people and her ability to communicate with the dead.

Yet here she was once again feeling a burden of guilt being carried by someone who had lost a loved one.

The gift of empathy is draining as around other people who comes with a lot of baggage. The thirty year old wife of a systems analyst found herself at times not willing to leave her home.

The seemingly frazzled housewife's radar zeroed in on an attractive Nubian subject standing tall in beige ankle wrapped four inch heels in the produce department.

She was a lithe stylish young woman sporting blue jean leggings paired with a white off-the-shoulder all cotton blouse. The heavy silver chained necklace hanging from an elegant neck supported by slender shoulders rested comfortably between two perfectly shaped cone breasts.

The woman's auburn tinted hair was pulled up in a French knot on top of her head. Silver dangling earrings hung from small pierced ears.

Amanda's assignment was consumed in choosing a ripe melon piled high on a table.

The slightly pointed nose with a slight hump twitched with uncertainty as the woman sniffed one melon then another. Small tapered fingers manicured with red lacquered nail polish were no match for the sizeable organic fruit as she tried squeezing the object of her attention.

Stephanie Irene Willis irritatingly allowed the melon to fall with a resounding thud before choosing another.

Suddenly, in a quick glance of her surroundings her brown eyes locked eyes with Amanda who was staring questionably in her direction. Amanda approached her subject.

"E-excuse me, I don't mean to stare, but I see an aura around you and I believe I-I'm feeling your sadness." Amanda said with understandable hesitancy.

Another perspective fruit fell among the cache of carefully stacked melons. A sense of skepticism quickly overcame the unsuspecting target's demeanor.

Stephanie questionably looked around before she directed her attention back to the brazen character standing before her.

"Are you talking to me?" She looked around once again finding it hard to believe what she had just heard.

"Why yes, yes I am." Amanda said this time with more clarity. "You have to let it go. You must stop blaming yourself."

"What do you mean? You don't know me!"

The confusion and disbelief on Stephanie's face was enough to garner an explanation.

"I'm sorry; I'm an Empath. I sense people's pain and sadness. Whenever I get this feeling I have to act on it." The clairvoyant said with renewed vigor.

"You lost your sister recently and you're carrying a heavy feeling of guilt. Am I correct?"

Understandably, the question received no response, but was only afforded the most wide-eyed stare of disbelief.

"She, I mean your sister, has stepped forth. She says to let you know it was not your fault."

"My-my sister?" Stephanie was in shock. "What do you mean? My sister is dead!" She stifled a sob that was beginning to rise up.

"I know that. And I'm sorry." Amanda said. "Let me explain."

"Yes! I think you'd better because this is some cow manure and it's crazy!"

"I'm an Empath with medium tendencies. Do you know what that is?"

Stephanie looked long and hard at the stranger standing before her. For the first time, Stephanie's eyes were drawn to the jelly stain on the woman's pink blouse.

Her hair was an unkempt mess and the kaki Capri's had seen better days. The child seated in the cart didn't appear to be feeling well. That alone may have accounted for the woman's disheveled appearance.

Amanda shifted uneasily as she watched her subject take in her appearance from head to toe. Fully knowing she was in need of a pedicure her toes nervously twitched in the well worn thongs.

"N-no, I don't know what that is." Stephanie finally uttered. "But, if I'm right you're going to tell me. Am I right?"

"Well… I'm sort of new at this medium thing. Then as an Empath, I haven't yet learned how to block out other people's emotions. I felt your sadness and saw the aura surrounding you, it let me know you were the one."

"W-what; you saw what?"

"Let's just say I saw a light surrounding your body. It was discernible to me because of my special sensibilities."

"Well…okay, if you say so, but it all sounds spooky and weird to me; if you don't mind my saying."

"I'll be the first to admit it's definitely something out of the ordinary. I just accept the fact that's it's a skill that can benefit others."

"How so? Please explain."

"I pick up on other people's energy. And when I do, the matter that is bogging that person down will manifest itself in given ways."

There was an aura surrounding you and that tingling sensation I always get when someone is about to come through happened."

"So now you see lights everywhere; is that it?"

"No, not everywhere, and not all the time; thank God." Amanda exclaimed.

"It would be too draining. In your case, you're feeling some kind of way about your sister's death."

A sharp intake of breath coming from Stephanie was an indication of proof.

A sound of shattering glass could be heard from the next aisle over.

Amanda smiled; fully satisfied her supernatural instincts were once again proven accurate. She watched amusingly as a look of shock, then a look of skepticism played across the trembling woman's face.

"Clean-up on aisle four" soon resonated over the intercom, breaking into the tense moment.

"I can sense your doubt in what I'm telling you." Amanda seriously added.

The defiant look on the woman's face confirmed her assumption.

So, the Empath offered a word of proof to help convince her disbelieving subject.

"Would it help if I told you your sister also witnessed the supernatural encounter you had days earlier with the spirit of the biblical vixen, Mrs. Potiphar?"

A sharp gasp escaped Stephanie's lips.

"Oh my! You know about that?"

"Glenda, your sister says to tell you that Etta Mae and her friend Tonika also told you the truth, but you didn't believe them either."

Stephanie grasped the table of melons for support nearly upending the entire cart in the process.

As if the disconcerting experience of encountering the likes of a biblical vixens wasn't enough, now she learns her deceased sister was a witness to the whole fiasco.

Stephanie remembered the day to be intriguing. After entering the bus she remembered feeling as if her life would never again be the same.

And if today was any indication I was correct she thought.

Now she has to deal with yet another creepy episode of the macabre-kind.

"Your sister, I believe stepped forth to relieve you of the sense of guilt you're having."

The astounding words the woman spoke finally hit home. Tears began to flow down the flawless face.

"She said to tell you the whole outcome of that night was totally her fault." Said Amanda.

The memory of a premonition of unshakable doom had run foremost in her mind all that unforgettable week.

She hadn't wanted Glenda to go out that Saturday night and had adamantly insisted she not go.

"Oh, Sissy." Glenda had said after giving her baby sister a reassuring hug. As she kissed her sister's face she could tast the salty tears her sister had shed.

"Don't worry…I'll be just fine. I'll tell you all about my night when I get home; okay?"

"You promise? I'll wait up."

"I promise! You silly goose." Glenda had joyfully responded.

But she hadn't been fine. While leaving the night club she frequently visited at 1:00 in the morning, a stray bullet had cut her beloved sister's life short.

Oh! Stephanie thought. If only I'd been even more persistent in keeping her from going that night. My precious Glenda would be here with me today.

Amanda watched the constant flow of tears slide down the prominent cheekbones. The empathetic housewife readily offered a tissue she fished from her purse to the grieving woman.

It's never easy reopening old wombs of loss even though she hoped her special gift would lessen the woman's grief.

"Glenda is laughing and shaking her head." Amanda said to her grieving assignment. "She said had she known that night you had psychic powers she certainly would've stayed home. She says tell her not to worry; I'm at peace."

A relieving smile enlightened Stephanie's face as the lines of guilt began to fade.

About that time little Billie began squirming in the grocery cart. Amanda rubbed his head and pushed it against her chest.

"Well… Billie here is becoming more and more impatient by the minute so…"

Now that her work was done, the discrete diviner next mission was to stop wee-fingers from toppling the stacked rack of apples within his reach. She began to move away.

"I'm glad I was able to offer you some form of comfort."

"Oh, yes… yes, yes! And thank you." Stephanie said vigorously shaking the woman's hand. "And you've truly made a believer out of me. Good bye!"

The two strangers exchanged hugs, then parted ways. Both locked in their own thoughts as to what it all meant.

Stephanie had finally found a happy medium between all the guilt she'd been carrying over losing her sister to a senseless crime to finally being able to accept it.

A weight of a thousand bricks has been lifted from my shoulders. So peace is possible. She thought.

After her sister's death nervous anxiety had shown itself in the manner of her frantically talking in run-on sentences.

Stephanie now felt capable of carrying on coherent conversations that would allow others to get a word in edgewise.

And as for Amanda, the fatigued mother of two knew there would always be an air of skepticism about her clairvoyant abilities.

Even Jake, her husband, as supportive as he is was having trouble balancing their real world with his wife's paranormal world.

"Looks like another satisfied customer." Amanda murmured smiling that all too familiar smile.

She planted a quick motherly peck on the toddler's ruddy cheeks.

Amanda adjusted the lid of his Sippy cup while pushing the nearly empty cart toward the checkout.

"I know I haven't gotten everything I came in here for… oh well, it's time for Billie's nap so I may as well head home."

On the other hand as Stephanie distractedly rounded the corner of the pickle aisle a familiar face greeted her with open arms.

It was Mother Janice Baldwin, a matronly lady of the church. Mother Baldwin had worn her hair in the upturned flip forever. At least the ten years Stephanie had known her. Mother Baldwin sat next to her now deceased mother.

Only the abundant strands of gray running throughout the outdated do made the difference of then and now.

Mother Baldwin had the dubious honor of serving on the motherboard of the church. A board mostly composed of older faithful women who were looked upon as very godly ladies. These women served as an example to the people giving stability to the church.

They are regarded as mothers to the entire congregation and are addressed as "mother" and then their last name.

Amanda glanced back from her place in the checkout line in time to witness the impromptu greeting between the two.

"Go ahead girl, tell her all about it. After all, you deserve it."

She had left the attractive unsuspecting shopper with much to think about.

Billy's understandable impatience had worn thin as he began to whine and kick even more.

"Okay sweetie, I'm ready to get home too." The gifted mother pushed her cart with renewed vigor all the way out the building.

"How're you ba-bee?" The all-knowing matron asked. "I thought I recognized you when I went by. You've grown to be a beautiful woman."

Stephanie found herself at a loss for words. She never expected having to carry on a conversation so soon after receiving the shock of her life.

"O-Oh! Thank you Mother Baldwin!" She said.

Fortunately, she was able to recall lucid memories of her years as a young girl in her mother's church.

"I couldn't help but over hear the conversation you and that…well… shall I say, that strange woman was having a short while ago.

I tell you, I started-

"Did you? Oh my goodness!"

To think someone she knew had overheard the strange conversation was a bit disconcerting.

Now the drama begins. Stephanie thought to herself. A hidden eye roll was concealed behind an unsteady hand she raised to her face.

She quickly swallowed the lump of loathing making its way up her throat.

She thought Mother Baldwin to be friendly enough. She had no reason to dislike the woman.

The annoyance she was possibly feeling was due to the church gossip monger possibly knowing her inner most thoughts. She hadn't even been able to fully digest them herself.

"Babee, I'm so happy for you. It must give you such peace to know your sister don't blame you."

Stephanie wasn't really listening to what was being said. The overabundance of freckles haphazardly scattered around the portly built matron's face was too distracting for her to focus.

She found herself connecting the dots from here to there. But during the sweep of the woman's face Stephanie's eyes locked with Mother Baldwin's speckled green eyes.

Stephanie was suddenly snapped out of her stupor by the woman's direct stare.

"Now me on the other hand-

"I'm sorry Mother, but I can't talk about it right now, so…"

"Oh, ba-bee, I totally understand."

Suddenly Stephanie found herself enveloped in the biggest motherly hug. She felt the cushion of the ample breasts crush against her own. The embrace was soon broken.

"That woman's message shocked me to a point of dropping a jar of pickles on the floor."

A flashback of hearing a call for clean up on aisle four resonated in Stephanie's mind.

"That was you Mother Baldwin?"

Suddenly the awkward moment was lifted in the quiet. The two shared a laugh.

"Yes!" Mother Baldwin said. "And when she said she had a message from your sister who I know is dead; I almost fainted honey."

Mother Baldwin took a deep breath before continuing.

"Course I don't know why that sort of thing should surprise me though 'cause it's becoming so normal nowadays. Ain't it?"

"Yes Ma'am. It is."

Oh, here comes Mother Jenkins." Mother Baldwin waved to her friend coming up the aisle.

"Hi, Mother Baldwin. How're you?"

"I'm good, I'm good. Mother you remember Mildred King's daughter Stephanie don't you. She's all grown up now. Ain't she pretty?"

"Why yes, I do. She looks just like her mother."

Mother Jenkins reached out and shook the now anxious young lady's hand. Stephanie looked around for an escape route.

"How're you, honey? I haven't seen you for awhile. You know your mother kept you in church when you were little. Your mother sat on "the amen corner. I tell you never heard such singing and praying as she did." she said.

"She set the church on fire with her singing. Can you sing honey?

"No ma'am."

"Oh, well even you if can't, the Lord will receive your praise anyway."

"Yes ma'am."

"You know this ole world don't have anything to offer you, but I can offer you Jesus-

"Oh, I'm sorry ladies, excuse me, but I have to get home. It's time for my daughter to get home from school and I want to be there when she does."

Knowing she would be forever locked in a conversation with the two church ladies Stephanie proceeded to brush past the two when Mother Jenkins grabbed a hold of her arm.

"I know you do honey, but it's my job as a mother of the church to guide you young ladies. Don't forget we've been where you all are trying to go."

"That's true." Mother Baldwin agreed. "And if they would only listen it would prevent them from going down the wrong path. Hallelujah!"

Not to be prolonged, Stephanie stopped long enough to glean the motherly advice, but her mind was already on escaping.

"Thank you mothers, but I really do have to go."

Mother Jenkins relinquished her firm grip on the young woman's arm.

"Well… alright then ba-bee." She said. "But I would love to see you on Sunday morning. I'm sure Rev. Johnson's got a word just for you."

"Yes ma'am."

Stephanie stepped past the two portly matrons and rapidly made her way out the market. They watched her go.

Mother Baldwin whispered to her friend. "Chile… Rev. Johnson's not the only one that has a word for that young woman."

"Whaa; what do you mean Janice?"

"You haven't heard it from me, but I just happened to overhear a conversation one of those so called psychic women was having with Mother King's daughter."

"Say what?"

Mother Jenkins leaned on the grocery cart shifting her ample breast to rest on her arms.

Her ears were pricked to hear what her fellow Mother of the Church had in store to tell.

"Let's go over to the Starbucks counter and I'll fill you in."

The two hurriedly made their way to a fresh hot cup of cappuccino eager to begin their gossip session.

CHAPTER
Eight

*Do not forget to show hospitality
to strangers, for by so doing some people have
shown hospitality to angels without knowing it.
Hebrews 13:2 NIV*

"Sir, would you care for a Cola, Sprite, or waata'?"
The young red-headed flight attendant's Southern drawl was quite noticeable as she made her way down the aisle with her drink cart.

"No, I'm fine. Thanks."

The burly passenger seated on the aisle said with a shake of his head. The man ran his hand through thick blond hair that reached to his shoulders.

The attendant's Southern twang was enough to pull Delilah seated in the window seat vacant stare away from the Boeing 737's window.

Damien seated in the middle seat engrossed in his I-Phone also declined the offer for refreshments.

"No thank you. You care for anything honey?" Damien asked Delilah.
No, I don't care for anything."

She turned to stare out the window once again with a deep sign of discontentment.

"A-are you okay?" Damien asked with genuine concern.

Y-Yes, I'm okay." Delilah replied with a glance in his direction. "In fact eve-ry-thing's just pea-chie!"

I wonder what that's all about. The befuddled husband thought.

Damien thinking it best not to ask turned his attention once again to messages he'd receive on his I-Phone. The few days he had been away had thrown the bank advisor way behind.

At the *moment* Delilah*'s* thoughts *and* feelings were in direct alignment with the billowing clouds fragmented here and there.

Damien shut off his phone with a pronounced movement.

"Okay Delilah! What is it?" *He* asked shifting his six foot frame in the cramped seat.

"Talk to me." He continued. "I can clearly see you're here, but yet you're not here. So what's on your mind?"

The sound of a snort escaped the gentlemen who had fallen asleep seated next to the couple.

He had fallen asleep just that quickly. He abruptly shifted his torso his torso toward the isle and stretched out one leg.

An inch of space had suddenly become available with the man's shifting.

Damien was able to fully look at his wife as he took her hand.

"I know you've, I-I mean we, we've been through a lot and I want you to know I take full responsibility for it all——

"Don't!"

An obviously irritated Delilah shouted with her hand up. She quickly lowered her voice.

"I-I don't want to talk about anything right now!" She indicated with a whisper.

"So... please—— just, just——

"What do you mean?" An equally agitated Damien asked in a terse breathy whisper.

"I mean I just don't want to talk about it!" Delilah said again with emphasis.

Damien watched the small delicate hand drop once again in his wife's lap, but he wasn't ready to curtail the matter and proceeded with the questioning.

"I don't get it. What do you want from me?" He solemnly asked.

The question went unanswered it seems for an eternity as they both sat locked in their own tormented thoughts.

They had returned to the Smith's home after a night of love making that rivaled anything they'd each known before.

With a brief and stoic explanation to their hosts, Delilah had retrieved her belongings and had returned with her husband to the hotel. Two days later they boarded the plane for home.

"I just don't get it!" Damien continued on. "We have talked well into the night, and-and I thought we had somehow come to a conclusion."

He threw up both his hand in defeat while attempting to adjust his position in the confines of the too cramped space.

"Apparently, I was wrong in thinking we both had found a 'happy medium' as far as our future was concern."

"But…I guess I was wrong." He exhaled a long breath.

Delilah's vision was suddenly obscured by a rogue cloud the plane had entered. She sat up with a jolt.

Almost immediately the startled woman began to hear the familiar words of the Prophet Eli Cummings, the man in white.

A vision of that strange cloudy mist on a bright and sunny day suddenly materialized.

Delilah had found herself in front of a huge structure when a 'man of mystery' had spoken to her.

The man's words of wisdom and insight had miraculously calmed her troubled spirit.

"Even you, an agnostic," the man had said, "must know there's no sin too great or too small the blood of your Savior can't cover."

His statement had been in response to the openly blatant declaration she had made to him.

"I'll never forgive that traitor!" She had shouted.

"You just don't know what he did to me——to our marriage!"

But the flagrant outburst hadn't surprised the man of mystery in the least.

He had merely sat quietly before saying to her.

"You my dear have much soul searching to do."

Delilah also recalled her reaction to the words that had followed as the man rose to leave.

"I pray you peace, and I pray you understanding." He had said.

In a panic state she had restrained her new found friend from leaving. He just couldn't desert her now that her mind was still a myriad of emotions.

I pray you peace and understanding. She had allowed the words to resonate in her spirit, hoping to somehow make sense of it all.

Delilah thought she had once found that peace and that understanding the man was speaking of while she laid in her husband's arms the last few days. Maybe it was all just a dream. She thought.

Am I really capable of such forgiveness? She thought as she twisted the elegant rock on her left ring finger.

A deeply concerned husband watched his wife's countenance closely.

I wonder what's going on in that mind of hers. Wait! Was that a hint of a smile?

But little could the errant but apologetic Damien comprehend that under the facade of indifference was beating a heart primed for breaking once again.

As for the despondent Delilah, the hint of a smile that had appeared was spurred on by the vision.

She felt herself falling at the prophet's feet and taking a hold of a 'nail scarred' hand as she openly wept.

"Oh, Lord… c-can you ever forgive me?" She had uttered.

Then she had heard the most beautiful words ever spoken.

"My Child, I never tire of forgiving you. In fact I intercede on your behalf daily." The transfigured man had spoken.

"Now you go and do likewise."

Even now she could feel herself being engulfed with the warm feeling of contentment.

A wayward daughter had received her own soul salvation on that fateful day.

Enough uncontrollable tears of joy and gratitude had rained down her cheeks to fill a stream; on that day.

Now she was feeling tender warm arms embrace her with reassuring love

Delilah looked up into the most concerned and caring eyes looking down into hers as she surrendered to the loving gesture.

She allowed herself to rest against the strong chest of her compassionate husband.

"Honey?" She said, lifting herself up to fully see his face.

"Yes dear?"

"I now truly know my——and your Redeemer lives."

She cupped his smoothly shaven chin into her hands.

The astounded look on his face prompted her to further explain.

"It's like this." She said. "Forgiveness comes easily at times, even for our grievous and painful hurts we endure.

But that's not to say many times, we are powerless to forgive in and of ourselves. No matter how hard we try."

She watched his face intently as an air of understanding began to surface.

"Awww... now I see."

"But... I've since learned this is when God's forgiving grace has the opportunity to touch and change us all. Do you understand?"

"Wow..." Damien was finally able to say after a long pause. "That's profound."

The thought of receiving unparalleled forgiveness for the unwarranted hurt and pain he had put his faithful 'help meet' through was astounding.

He was gathered in on his own thoughts thinking of his own prayer of repentance.

After the phantom man 'Adam' revealed to him his father's wishes from the 'beyond' he was never the same again.

That prayer had bought such a sense of peace and deliverance in him that true humility had flooded his soul.

After leaving the Smith's home the only thing he wanted to do was humble himself before his wife and before God.

After a short time Damien said to Delilah.

"I asked you on our first night back together to forgive me for all the hurt I had put you through."

"Yes. Y-you did, but——

No, now hear me out." Damien said putting his finger to his wife's lips. "But all you could say then was that you needed time."

"Yes, I did say that." Delilah responded.

"A-and I'm sorry I couldn't give you a more definitive answer at the time, but just as we went through that rogue cloud, I was reminded of a conversation——

"The one with the Prophet."

Delilah cast a wide-eyed glance his way before countering.

"Yes… with the Prophet; the Prophet, Jesus Christ!"

"I see."

Damien said this more to himself than to his wife.

"I can't afford to clog my spirit any longer with un-forgiveness after experiencing something like that."

"Thank you Jesus!" Damien shouted. "To God be the glory! I'm truly grateful."

Their seat mate awoke with a start and stared intently at his two neighbors.

"Ooh! Sorry."

Damien said uttering an acute apology before turning once again to his wife.

"And I've also denied the Lord far too long. I can't describe the relief I felt when I asked Him to come into my life and to forgive me of my sins."

"You know what?" Delilah asked. "Forgiveness is like a caged bird is finally set free."

"I know it's hard——

"No, no, it's not hard." Delilah stated emphatically.

"On our own, it's hard, but it is only through His Holy Spirit that we're able to be free."

Damien received the words with open abandonment with a shake of his head in agreement.

"But…honey," Delilah said intently watching his expression.

"I want you to know my forgiveness does not mean I deny your responsibility in hurting me, nor does it minimize or justify all the wrong you did."

"What? Damien said with a startled look. "But-but——

Delilah's raised hand cut his rebuttal off mid-sentence.

"No, now you hear me out." She continued. "How-ev-er, through my new found relationship with Jesus Christ; I can forgive you without excusing your wrong doing."

Damien abruptly let go of his wife's hand and closed his eyes while allowing the bulk of her words to sink in.

"You know what baby." He lovingly said. "What you just said means a lot to me."

"It does; you truly mean that?" Delilah asked with a tad uncertainty.

"Yes, it does. And I know it will take a lifetime for me to make it up to you, but I'll spend a lifetime trying."

At the very moment her inner spirit leapt for joy hearing his words of humility.

"That's why I can say to you and everyone!" Delilah shouted with loud jubilant laughter. "I know my Redeemer lives!"

"No, you forgot!" Damien said joining in the elation.

"Our Redeemer lives!"

Their exuberant outburst caused a stir amongst their fellow passengers.

Some willingly received the declaration, while it left others with a sense of irritation.

But, most surprisingly, the declaration of redemption was well received by the passenger seated next to the jubilant couple.

However, notwithstanding, the fiery red haired attendant rapidly approached the liberated couple with disdain.

"Shhh!" she indicated with a finger to her lips. "Could you two please be more considerate?"

"Oh! We're sorry." Delilah offered apologetically. "We'll keep it down."

Having accepted the apology with a nod of her head the attendant retreated in the direction from which she had come.

Or, so they'll try. The now fully awake gentleman laughingly thought to himself.

"And to prove my deliverance from the web of immoral deceit I found myself in," Damien went on to add, "I'm going to do everything in my power to make your life as strife free as possible from this day forward."

"Your power won't be enough." How do I know you won't fall prey to that temptation again? Delilah interjected.

"Don't think your new found deliverance won't be put to the test, because the 'enemy' will make sure you'll be tempted every chance he can get."

"Humph!" Damien answered, nodding his head in agreement.

"No doubt; I very well may be, but you forgot one thing."

"And just what might that be sir?" Delilah coyly asked.

"He who began a good work in me is able to complete it until Jesus comes."

"Alright… that was a good one. I'll give you that. And don't forget you now have the *Fruit of the Spirit*.

And self-control is one of the fruit." His esteemed wife said. And with self-control you can tell your body "No; you don't control me; I control you." Delilah added.

Holy scriptures the new converts had either heard or had read in childhood was called to their remembrance like bullets of rapid fire.

"I guess there is something to be said about *"training up a child in the way he should go, and when he is old he will not depart from it."* Damien said.

"It's always there; we're never far from it. In the words of my mother who used to say to me;

"Son, the Lord's promise to you peace as children if you're *taught of the Lord; and great will be their peace.*

Well… she'd say, "I've done my part. You were taught of the Lord. But what you do with what you were taught is totally up to you."

"She's right, honey, because my grandma kind of said the same thing to Etta Mae, Cynthia and me.

We were taught of the Lord so our soul's salvation is not on her. She won't have to answer for any of our misdoings; they're all totally on us."

Damien was thinking about mothers and grandmothers and all their wisdom. He thought about the precious little nuggets they pass on to the '*fruit of their womb.*'

He thought how about how those *nuggets* truly are blessings if one is careful to hold on them.

He thought on the last nugget she gave to him before taking her last breath.

"You will become a part of the world. You will stray. I have no doubt. It's just what young people do." His mother had said.

"But I've asked the Lord to keep you until you come home."

"Keep me until I come home."

"What was that; keep you until you come home?" Delilah asked.

"Huh? Damien hadn't realize he spoken it audibly. So he repeated it to the understanding of his wife.

"Oh, it was something my mother said to me before she passed.

"Well you've certainly come home, brother!" Delilah said teasingly.

"Yes, I certainly have at that. And it's all because of my mother's prayer."

Delilah was at a loss for words and only shook her head in agreement for she had also come home because of a grandmother's prayer.

"And, so my dear!" Damien said to her. To put your and my mind at ease, whenever I feel a tug in my heart that makes me uncomfortable, like King David I'll ask the Lord to:

"Search me O' God and know my heart; try me and know my thoughts."

His wife's inquisitive nature took over as she sat absorbing the seriousness of her husband's tone.

The man is preaching! She wondered when he would accept his calling. She thought.

"W-where is that from?" Delilah asked. "I-I mean I know its scripture and all, but—

The future preacher playfully tweaked his wife's nose.

"That my dear is from Psalm 139. And King David went on to ask the Lord:

"See if there be some wicked way in me; cleanse me from every sin and set me free."

"And set me free…" Delilah repeated, pondering the phrase.

"And how do you know He did?"

She said this strictly for the sake of solidifying Damien's own faith in 'the Almighty.'

"I know, because as I prayed that scripture, somewhere in the recess of my spirit I heard the Lord remind me of the man in my father's church.

"Who? What man?" Delilah asked sitting up to look her husband in the face.

But she would never comprehend how much it pained him to reveal what he would say to her next.

"The man, w-who raped me.

"What? A man raped you? When?"

"When I was a young boy."

Damien said, clearing his throat.

"Honey, I had no idea… y-you never told——

"I know. I've never told anyone. It was my deepest darkest secret. But the Lord said I had to forgive the man."

"Well… did you?"

Delilah asked, feeling more compassionate than ever towards her husband.

"Did I what?"

"Did you, or have you rather forgiven that man?"

Damien rubbed clammy sweaty palms down the front of his slacks before he answered her question.

"Y-Yes!. That is… I would like to think I have."

The concerned and compassionate wife looked long and hard at the handsome man seated next to her.

She couldn't have loved him more than at that very moment.

"I remember feeling light as a feather after I said "He is forgiven" into the air. That's when I knew I had the indwelling of the Holy Spirit."

Damien added. "And At that very moment I believe I saw a dark figure lift from my body."

"Wow."

Wow was all she could utter.

The 'come to Jesus' discussion was resting heavily on Delilah's compassionate heart.

She had never heard that side of her husband's childhood. She gave his hand a reassuring squeeze. It was her only way of offering comfort and understanding.

"I'm sorry, honey. I'm sorry you had to suffer through that ordeal."

The remembrance of the horrific time in his life caused Damien to squirm uneasily in his seat.

He cleared his throat in a manner of stifling the flow of tears he felt welling up within him.

"Uh, uhlm... honestly honey, it-it's all good." He was finally able to stammer. "Sometimes life's just a bitch! That's all; just a bitch."

Damien fell silent. Delilah could only hope the renewed love she had for her now redeemed husband of nine years radiated through the contented smile plastered on her face.

The couple's closest neighbor seated next to Damien was feeling forlorn after overhearing the intense discussion.

"Yes," Damien continued, speaking more to himself than to anyone else. "I may've drawn a lemon, but thank God, He has given me Jesus, the sugar in my lemonade!"

The gentleman seated next to Damien shifted uncomfortably in his seat once again. The couple's life saga left him shaking his head.

"Whew! Ooh boy!" He said before getting up then rushing to relieve an urgent call of nature.

"I just know that I know I've been changed." Damien testified. "I'm feeling so at peace."

Delilah smiled up at her newly evenly-yoked husband without responding.

Just knowing the unconditional love of God was enough to sustain their concerted efforts in their newly formed walk with Christ brought a song to her remembrance.

"*I-I know I've been changed. I-I know I've been cha-anged; the angels in heaven done signed my name. You know the angels in a heaven done———*

"Now... let me ask you this!" Damien inquired, cutting her off in mid song. "How do you know that song?"

She responded by playfully grabbing a hold of her husband's muscular bicep in both hands and resting her head on his broad shoulder.

"Grams" used to sing that song while she went about her day."

Then as a sudden thought came to her mind, she added.

"Humph. That's funny. I wonder why I'm just now remembering it."

By now, the ruddy complexioned, blond haired, blue-eyed, six foot gentleman had returned to his seat.

But as for the two, they were now seated in blissful silence with peaceful smiles on each of their faces.

The gentleman was truly thankful the distressing conversation had finally come to an end.

It's often said; *"there is joy in the presence of the angels of God who are the friends and neighbors of Christ."*

A major breakthrough had surely taken place in this now serene couple's lives.

Their seating arrangement had not been coincidental, nor was it by chance.

The angel 'Breakthrough' was the man seated in the connecting seat.

It also was no coincidence that Damien's room number had been changed from the first floor to the eighth floor. The angel had carried the errant man's bags to his new suite.

The angel Breakthrough also had a hand in the changed suite Damien was issued. In that as the number eight is God's number for 'new beginnings.'

He was there to watch the circumcision of their hearts through Christ and their receiving of the Holy Spirit.

The angel's two assignments are now in Christ and are becoming new creations with godly characters being created by the power of God's Spirit.

Two of God's anointed have come home and will be a mighty source for revival in the kingdom.

The shackles of bondage, perversion, and disbelief are now broken.

The contented angel allowed a breath of fulfillment to escape from his smiling lips. He overcompensated by stretching two long legs into the center aisle.

"Yep! Everything is good here."

CHAPTER
Nine

*"I am the Resurrection and the life.
He who believes in me will live even though he dies..."*
John 11:25KJV

"What the— I be damn it if I don't have a darn mole in my freaking yard!"

The Smith's home have been guests free for about a week. So the dedicated lawn keeper had ample time to do what he enjoyed most; that is other than golf. Landscaping.

The in-laws, his wife's sister and husband were back in New York prayerfully on the mend. He knew his wife was still skeptic about the supposed reconciliation. Yet she was prayerful. She had told him once; my sister is going to be who she is; her own person." So she had kept quiet about the whole situation.

Now Donnie's attention is drawn to his front yard as he stood surveying the extensive damage. Wishing above all hope the damage was done by a lone rodent.

Unfortunately, upon further inspection, evidence of more damage became apparent which left the homeowner irate.

"Well I'll be damn! Just look at my lawn! I can't catch a break. If it's not that… fish-stealing fur-ball; it's a freaking damn mole or moles!"

No one took more pride in their landscaping abilities than Donnie Leroy Smith.

The meticulous care he took of his horticultural skills was enough to rival the Chauncey Heights Golf Course. And he knew where every crevice and knoll was at that place.

Had it not been such overkill, a Japanese Koi pond would be gracing his front lawn as well as it did the back yard.

"Well hi'dee, hi'dee ho'neighbor!"

Donnie looked up in time to see John Reid stepping into his yard.

The man's jovial greeting broke into his distraught neighbor's thoughts as he stood spread-eagled with folded arms. Donnie shouted aloud.

"And it looks like it happened overnight!"

He threw up both his hands in anguish as his heart thumped wildly against his chest. "I pity the fool" at the end of that fury. John said. "S'up my man!"

Donnie responded giving his neighbor the usual hand dap.

"I can't catch a break. I can't believe this crap man!"

"Oh wow! I see why you're so upset."

John kicked at the loosened sod with his foot.

"Damn! You're right, that's some serious damage."

"Ya' think!" Donnie retorted. "All I know it's the last thing I need about now. Damn it!"

The desponded bystander felt compelled to offer some form of reasoning seeing the full anguish his neighbor was in.

"Well… perhaps the recent rains produced an overabundance of grubs. So you know—

His remarks was cut mid stride before the infuriated homeowner added.

"Yeah, yeah, I know, mole hills and tunnels do major damage… believe me; I know. I'm looking at it."

"True, true, but what I was going to say is sometimes mole control is not about grub control, but you have to make sure grubs aren't behind the invasion."

He hadn't received a response so he quietly added.

"You'll just have to make it unpleasant for the bastards and spray your yard with a castor oil concoction."

Donnie looked at John with an air of suspicion.

"What do you know about getting rid of moles?"

"O-only that I had them earlier and—"

"You what! You mean this could be your mole you ran in my yard!"

"Oh, no, no way, man. It couldn't be my mole."

John took a step backwards shaking his head in denial.

"And why is it you're so sure?"

"Be-cau-zz, man! I killed the damn thing myself!"

His reply caught the irate groundskeeper off guard. So he asked looking at his neighbor with full skepticism.

"And just how did you do that?"

"Well, you won't believe this, but I was standing in my yard the other day and I saw the grass was moving. "What da' heck! I thought."

"And check this out!"

The recaptured action is done in animated movements.

"It just so happens I had a pitchfork in my hand so I stuck it in the ground where the grass was moving. And… wah la! Up came this big squirming star nosed mole!"

"Damn dude, that had to freak you out."

"I wasn't so much freaked out as I was if I hadn't gotten the sucker!"

John chuckled.

"Now as for my girls; wife included… it was a different story."

"Don't tell me. My girl Mac chewed you a good one for sticking a pitchfork in that critter?"

Donnie laughed a hearty laugh. The run-in he'd had with the little animal rights avenger was still fresh in his mind.

"She is too much."

"You know it! Hell hath no fury like my little munchkin when it comes to defending animals!"

The shared laughter echoed down the street as they thought of the little crusader's fervor for animal protection.

"You don't have to tell me. She sure chewed my butt a good one over that Miss Gretchen's cat last week."

"I heard about that." John said, snickering. "And she still keeps an eye out to make sure it stays out of your yard."

"Did you mend that hole?"

"What hole?"

"The hole she pinky swore she'd get you to mend."

Donnie looked at his neighbor's face for some sort of recognition, but found none.

"We did do a pinky-swear you know."

"Can't help you there bruh."

"Oh well…it's probably for the best. I got a feeling I'll be seeing that ole fur ball again then."

They both laughed as they are soon joined by Josh, their neighbor from across the street.

"Say brothers; what're you guys up to?" Before anyone could answer, Josh's eyes followed the trail of uprooted grass.

"Oh, you don't have to tell me. I can see what's happening before my eyes; mole damage."

Nothing needed to be said. As the three men stood observing the extensive damage Josh looked up and saw a hearse followed by a line of cars proceeding down the street.

"Hey! Look guys here comes a funeral."

All eyes turned toward the approaching funeral procession lined with cars as far as eyes could see.

"Wonder whose funeral that is." Josh said under his breath as if speaking louder would somehow disturb the solemnest of the moment.

Donnie pondered for a bit, then suddenly snapped his fingers and said.

"That's got to be Lawrence Russell's funeral. Man, you know, he said particularly to John. "They said he came back from Iraq with horrendous wombs to most parts of his body. Remember?"

"Oh! That's right!" A light of recollection suddenly snapped on in John's brain. And if I recall, the man never fully recovered from taking that piece of shrapnel in his neck."

"Come on you guys! How could he just now be dying from that?" Josh asked unbelievingly. "If it's who I think it is it's been at least two to three years since he returned from over there."

"Precisely our point!"

The two patriotic veterans said simultaneously fully knowing there's no time limit on body trauma when it comes to healing.

Their undivided attention was once again given to the somber event unfolding before them.

The police escort had rushed ahead of the hearse, clearing the way for the procession. The flag draped coffin could be seen through the hearse's window. The three men watched with heartfelt compassion.

Donnie and John both stood at attention and offered a salute out of respect for a fellow soldier. Both had served in the armed forces; Donnie the United States Army, and John, the United States Air Force.

The motorcade rolled on coming from the 'Re-dig the Wells of Jubilation' Worship Center where the service had been held was now making its way to the cemetery. The mourners with contrite hearts sat in their respective vehicles looking straight ahead.

The entourage lasted a good ten minutes. When the last car had made its way past the onlookers standing with their hand over their hearts, a female voice broke into the silence.

"How so?"

The question was in response to what Josh had uttered before they fell silent.

"I'll tell you how. It's because trauma patients are more often than not, seriously injured with multiple body regions imaginable! The damn fools over there do everything in their power to inflict as much bodily damage and dismemberment as possible!"

"You know what... you're right." Donnie added. "And sometimes the soldiers commit suicide because they're hurting so bad, or got so hooked on Opioids they don't know night from day"

"I sure hope that wasn't the case with Lawrence." John said. "I knew when he was deployed there was a slight chance of him making it."

"Why wouldn't he make it? If that's the case, why would any of them make it?" Donnie said agitatedly.

Then Josh chimed in.

"Whatever it was that did him in it looks like it worked on him slowly. And, I just believe the government is in denial when it comes to our wounded warriors, if you ask me."

"Well, no one asked you!" John surprisingly retorted in defiance. "I'm a veteran and I'm sure "Uncle Sam" knows what he's doing.

He proceeded to pull out a set of military dog tags he's worn since departing from the Air Force some years ago.

It was only by habit he wore them as they had been a part of daily regimen for over ten years. He hadn't served a full twenty year term by attending college. He was eager to get established in a technology related career.

But that didn't stop the veteran from once again snapping to attention with a salute and shouting with pride; "God Bless America!"

In fact, all parties involved couldn't help but stand up for patriotism.

"Well…it looks as if we're all in safe hands with 'Mr. Give Me Liberty, or Give Me Death' here defending our country."

Josh jokingly slapped John on the shoulders.

"Just kidding; I'm proud of you man. Thanks for your service. Oh! And you too Mr. Smith."

"You're welcome son. It was the least I could do for my country. It was an honor to serve."

Donnie shook his head in agreement. He wiped away an escaping tear.

The three were so engrossed in the conversations they had not seen or heard Etta Mae standing silently watching the scenario being played out before her.

The somber moment was broken by Donnie in his assessment of the situation.

"Well he doesn't have to worry about his ailments anymore, because like the song says; *He's a new born soldier; gone on ho-me.*"

"What!" Donnie asked jovially referring to his impromptu song rendition.

"Now I know you guys have heard that song by Shirley Caesar."

"Spare us the pain man… and leave the singing to your girl, Shirley!" Josh said slapping John's open palm. They all roared with laughter.

Donnie suddenly turned to see his wife standing behind him. He cleared his throat.

"Honey! How long have you been standing there? We were just— He said this all while advancing toward his wife for a quick hug and peck on the lips.

Even the other two shifting nervously at having been caught off guard managed a meek greeting.

"Oh! Well hello there."

"H-hi Etta Mae, I didn't hear you come up." Josh sheepishly said.

"Hello guys, I didn't mean to startle you, but I saw the funeral procession from the window. I had fully intended to go, but I missed it."

"You mean you knew him Etta Mae?" John asked.

"Not him personally, but I know his sister Margaret. She worked at Bethany Memorial Hospital where I used to work."

"Plus, don't forget she's also a member of our church." Donnie added.

"You're right, honey. I very seldom got to talk to her at church, but you're so right."

Even though she was still miffed at herself for having missed her former co-worker brother's funeral she soon found herself being amused by the jovial camaraderie happening between the three neighbors.

"But yeah." Donnie said. "I know what you're saying man. My boy was sick for a very long time. And from the looks of it he never got over it."

The callous remark earned him a slap on the back of his head by his astonished wife.

"Donnie! Don't be so heartless."

Now rubbing the back of his head, Donnie leaned over once again and pecking her cheek offered an apology.

"Sorry honey. You were right. That wasn't a nice thing to say."

"Well, duhhh!"

John now feeling a bit whimsical himself, said. "Not from the looks of it! After all 'dem hearse wheels do just keep on a rolling!"

"You guys! Show some respect!" Etta Mae laughingly shouted. "I know they say we should *"rejoice when someone goes home, but morn when a child is born,"* but, I…I just feel so awful."

"Do they really say that?" Josh asked. "Not to cut you off Etta Mae."

"It's quite alright Josh. In fact, I would like to hear the answer myself Mr. Reid!"

"Yes! Gregg Allman said it or sung it rather." John said, "In fact, as they say in the Bible; you're supposed to "rejoice when people die and mourn when they're born." Why? I guess because the most painful acts you go through in life is being born, and then having to die."

"Ah, not to bust your sermonic bubble dude, but I believe that was 'Credence Clear Water Revival.' And it wasn't a hearse keep on rollin;' it was 'big wheels' keep on rollin.'

Besides… what would a metal rocker know about what the Bible says anyway?" Donnie jovially asked.

"I didn't say he knew anything; I said it was said in the Bi—

"Honey, he's right." I heard, or at the least read in Ecclesiastes 7:1, where it said:

"A good name is better than fine perfume, and the day of death better than the day of birth."

"Oh, lawd! The 'Bible-thumper' cometh!"

A sudden collective gasp was heard among the group. The callous remark had earned the humorous husband yet another playful slap on the old noggin. They all laughed.

But not to be outdone the subject soon became focused on the deceased man, only this time it was in reference to his soul.

"Well… I just hope he got it together with the Lord Almighty. The dude, I-I mean Russell, if I recall was known to be a smack-daddy in his hey-day." Donnie added.

"I wouldn't know if he did or didn't." Josh piped in. "For one, I didn't know the man so…"

John looked upon Donnie's callous remark with disdain.

"Man! I can't believe you. Now why're you pulling up the dead man's past, dude?"

"Don't get me wrong bro; I don't mean no disrespect, but me and my wife know his sister Margaret. She's also a member of our church. So I know for a fact she was on the man to give his life to the Lord."

"Hel-lo-o!" Etta Mae said deciding to chime into the derailed conversation.

"I believe that hearse was coming from that church over on Sprawling Street. So, apparently without your consent, Mr. Smith he must've joined somebody's church."

"And I bet our girl Margaret was right there praying for her brother to the end!"

Etta Mae only rolled her eyes at the absurdity of her husband's humorous remark.

The two bystanders thought this would be a good time as any to shake the melancholy mood of the hour.

"Say," John began saying, "imagine what would've happened if while his sister was praying; the man died. But, all of a sudden he sets up and shouts? "Whatz-up, Sis!"

Just the thought of that happening bought Josh much needed laughter. But as for Etta Mae and Donnie, it was no laughing matter.

"And you don't believe that could happen?" Etta Mae asked the two.

"O' ye of little faith."

"Oh! So I take it you've both seen somebody return from the dead?" John asked.

"Well... John-Boy," Josh said amusingly with a slap to the man's shoulder. "I guess you're the only one among us that hasn't had a close encounter of the 'spirit kind.'

"A-a what-encounter?" John asked with a furrowed brow.

"My friend," Josh said. "We each standing here have had supernatural encounters with spirits of the Bible-kind."

The stunned neighbor looked to the husband and wife team for confirmation and was obliged when they both shook their heads in unison.

"Well, I'll be damned." John said.

"Yeah, man," Josh continued. "Just last week, I was helped by a man dressed entirely in white after a bullet grazed my temple."

The fortunate survivor began to choke up just recanting the close call he'd suffered.

"After the man helped me to a city bench, I suddenly found myself pouring out my soul to this stranger. And man; before I knew it, I was on my knees repenting. And when next I looked up, the man was gone; Just like that."

"Wow!" It was all John could muster to say.

It was now the Smith's turn to share. And if that wasn't enough, our encounters began in our home."

"You mean spirits showed up in your house? No way!"

"Yes, that's what we mean brother." Donnie confirmed. "It all started with the woman 'Eve' speaking with Etta Mae and Tonika, Josh's wife."

Yes, and they even followed me and Tonika out to the mall. Well… not followed us but"

"And if that wasn't enough, tell 'im about who your wife met on her way home, brotha' man!

"On yeah…Tonika met the 'Adulterous Woman' of the Bible on her way home a few days ago."

It soon became apparent the confessions were beginning to be a bit too much for their bewildered neighbor.

"There's no way am I going to stand here and believe that crap! And you guys are some damn fools if you think I would."

"Well, suit yourself," Etta Mae joined in, "but we were just warning you not to be surprised if and when it happens with you."

"Now just let me get this straight." John said still not convinced. "You're telling me that in tow thousand and seventeen supernatural visitations by long ago spirit beings are happening? Now! Right now, in these times?"

"Yep," Etta Mae said. "That's exactly what we're saying. And from the looks of it, no one appear to be exempt."

"But, keep in mind," Donnie chose to add. "They're not just any spirits; we said 'biblical,' meaning staunch figures from the Bible."

Suddenly, there was no need for further explanation as low and behold, for catching the neighbor's attention were two figures approaching them from the south dressed in the fashions of biblical times.

The one in the lead was clothed in a long scarlet loose fitting garment overlaid with a navy drape. The onlookers could see that her feet were shod with dark leather sandals each time she took a step. On her arm she carried a basket filled with fruits and veggies. What appeared to be a loaf of bread extended from the basket.

The basket was obviously heavy seeing as how she would switch the load from one arm to the other. With one free hand she reached up to tuck loose strands of dish- water blond hair underneath the folds of a black head scarf that reached her shoulders.

The one lagging behind was attired in pretty much the same manner. She walked at a much slower pace, evidently engrossed in reading a papyrus scroll she had in her hand.

Assessing the situation, Etta Mae and Donnie, as well as Josh knew right away what they'd just spoken of was coming to fruition at that very moment.

"Well tell the truth and shame the devil!" Etta Mae emphatically stated. All eyes watched uneasily as the two phantom figures approached.

The woman in the lead anxiously looking behind her, called to the slower one.

"Come on MARY! Hurry up! Lord, if that girl walked on coals her feet are sure to disintegrate. She's never in a hurry; always reading and pondering!"

The woman talked on in a never-ending banter, leaving the onlookers in awe.

Even in her hurried gait the phantom's thoughts returned to the evening their friend, Jesus had finally paid them an expected visit.

Even when we had Jesus over for dinner, I'm busy, busy, preparing meals and cleaning the house. And what did my sister do? Sat at His feet. Sat at his feet mind you; All day! I mean she was hanging onto the Lord's every word.

Of course I couldn't blame her, because if I hadn't been so busy I would've sat down there myself."

Hmm, come to think of it, I shouldn't have complained about it though, because Jesus said "she was doing what was right and I shouldn't be anxious about things that didn't matter."

Well! I thought eating mattered! But, it seems the food my sister was eating was far more fulfilling than any food I could prepare.

By now the biblical specters had reached the watching humans. Needless to say, John found himself backing away.

Donnie and Josh simultaneously reached out to restrain his exit. Donnie said to the frightened man.

"Oh no you don't, my man. You didn't believe us when we told you. So now you get to experience it for yourself!"

"Sister!" Come on now, girl! I swear if she was any slower!"

Then she noticed she had an audience.

"Oh! I'm sorry; hello sirs a-and madam."

She felt a bit embarrassed.

"Y-you're probably wondering who I am…or who we are. Am I right?"

The perplexed group all shook their heads in agreement and looked from one to the other shrugging their shoulders. Donnie was the first to speak up.

"Well, we were sort of wondering… in fact, I was just tell—

"I'm Martha, Martha of Bethany.'

The woman glanced in the direction of her sister once again who is steadily advancing.

"Oh, finally! My sister; the slow one."

The onlookers followed her gaze as the lagging sibling arrived with her head buried in a papyrus.

"I'm sorry, but this is my sister; M-ary who is for-ev-er reading those scrolls.""

Martha reached for the scrolls hoping to gain her sister's undivided attention.

"Sister, please get your head out of that scroll, and say hello to these fine humans."

Mary successfully dodging her sister's grasp, looked up from her scroll just long enough to speak, but quickly returned to her reading.

"Hello."

Martha exhaled a long sigh. She shook her head in disbelief and turned her attention to the onlookers once again.

"And I can see you've been watching a funeral. But can I just tell you all about a funeral Mary and I attended?"

"Well…yes you may." Etta Mae said, already knowing the woman's story. "You okay with it honey… Josh, John, you both okay?"

"Okay by me." Donnie responded.

Josh was the next to speak.

"Hey, fine by me. I somehow believe she's going to anyway, so…"

John remained silent.

"Thank you. I shall be brief."

Mary cast an unbelieving glance in her sister's direction as she begins her tale.

"You see, it was a funeral for our beloved brother, Lazarus who had fallen ill. We'd sent for our good friend, Jesus… whom we just knew could cure our brother of his ailment."

"Well… yeah!" Etta Mae interjected. "That's why we call Him *Jehovah Rapha*; *"the Lord God that healeth thee!"* Even we know that."

"Honey, just allow the wo—I mean Martha to tell the story, please." Donnie said. Etta Mae conceded but not before throwing her beloved spouse a daggered look.

Martha smiled and resumed her tale.

"As I was saying, it's not like we hadn't seen Jesus cure a blind man, a cripple, and a—

"Yea, yea, just get to the point sister; we sent for Jesus…"

"Ooh! And we thought she was the quiet timid one." Donnie said under his breath. He nudged John who was standing nearby.

"Oh! Now she finds her voice."

Martha cast a penetrating stare toward her disruptive sibling.

"An-ywa-ay… our friend, Je-sus, didn't come. Or he didn't come when we first called for him. So, my brother died."

Obviously distraught she paused for a moment as if being choked up.

"Well; now it was too late, or so we thought. Now, am I right sister?"

Still engrossed with reading, Mary peered up long enough to address Martha's comments.

"Sister, you may have thought it, but I knew better. Did you forget at whose feet I sat?"

Martha's response to her sister was a bit confrontational.

Yes, you're right. I am aware of whose feet you sat. How could I forget! And I tell you something else; I believe you hurt your friend's feelings when you repeated what I had just said to Him.

Mary's head shot up after that remark.

"When I repeated what you had said?"

"Yes!"

Martha emphatically answered.

"Well please tell me exactly just what you said that I supposedly repeated it."

The captured audience stood silently by watching. Eight sets of eyes looked from one specter to the other as their engaging dialogue continued.

"I had said to Him, "Lord, if only you had been here my brother wouldn't have died.""

Mary gasped.

"You mean you said that to Him too! Oh no."

She covered her face and wept. Just the thought of Jesus, her most trusted friend having to hear her unbelief; let alone that of Martha's was too painful.

"Yes… I'm sorry to say but that was pretty much the first thing I said to Him. I-I just didn't know."

But, Martha was too deep into her own pain. She watched Mary's head bow in sorrow.

"That must be why my Lord actually groaned in His spirit. Then He wept."

Tears began to trickle down the heart broken face.

"All because of me…I'm so sorry my friend."

"Awww… Mary don't weep."

Martha feeling anguished embraced her despondent sister in a quick reassuring hug.

"Stress is bad for your physical and mental health."

She lifted the hem of her garment and dabbed away the tears running down Mary's face.

"And it's also making you an unhappy sister. Besides, it's possible our friend wept not only because of your weeping; He probably wept because you, me and all those paid mourners were sobbing like nobody's business!"

"Duhh!"

Etta Mae had a hard time keeping quiet.

"Don't you get it? He was or is rather such a compassionate friend… I'm sure that's all it was."

The men were all shaking their heads in agreement.

"Oh! And just how do you figure that Etta Mae!"

Martha retorted, annoyed by the human's verbal intrusion.

"I don't think so."

Then she said solely to her sister.

"Remember Mary, Jesus personally sent for you even after I was the one who ran out to meet Him.

"Yes, Sister, I remember you coming to get me. It's just that I think it was because He knew how much I loved and spent time with—

"That you should've known better; is that it? Well, I loved Him too, but I just had things to do. That's all. So I couldn't just sit at His feet all day like you!"

Mary raised her hand as if to stop the onslaught she knew was coming. She had heard it all before.

"Yes you did, and when I ran out, I pushed past you so fast, I forgot to say thank you."

Mary turned and bowed to her superior sister.

"Thank you for all you do, have done and will continue to do. I just had a lot on my mind at the time, you know."

Now it was Donnie's time to intercede.

"I could be wrong, but it seems to me, Mary, you yourself were a bit miffed at your dear friend. Now, I'm sorry, but that's just the way I read and saw the thing."

All heads turned to look at Donnie, staring in disbelief at his boldness. Martha feeling the need to come to her little sister's defense responded by saying.

"Well it may interest you to know we both were at the time. But had we known Jesus purposely stayed away in order His Father would be glorified by raising our brother from his sleep, then neither of us would've been.

However, Mary groaned and covered her mouth as a flashback of the Lord's actions gripped her psyche.

"Jesus shared so much with me! You're so right Martha. I don't blame you. So what if we buried our brother and four days later, He showed up. I should've known He was the Resurrection; it should've been me!"

"I'm sorry Martha, but I just have to say," Etta Mae begins, "I would've never pictured you as having been so nonchalant and so sarcastic over the matter."

"Hey, ladies," Josh said, now brazen enough to add his unwarranted input. "I hear what both of you are saying. But, did either of you ever stop to think that just maybe your love, your belief and your trust in the Lord was all He wanted?"

The complexity of Josh's statement stunned everyone involved and left each one searching their own hearts.

Martha, as usual, was the first to speak.

"Hummm…you know, you may be right. No wonder He said my sister was doing what was right by sitting at His feet. There I was trying to impress with all my scurrying, being busy."

Feigning tears, Martha encourages Mary to finish the story.

"But my sister can tell you the story better than I can. I get so choked up. Go on Mary, you tell them. Just the thought of it all just chokes me up."

Obviously, agitated, Mary began rolling up her beloved scroll. Then finally giving the onlookers her undivided attention she began recounting the story of her brother Lazarus and his miraculous resurrection.

"*You see people*; i*t all began with my Lord saying to my sister; "Your brother shall live again," and then with Martha saying; "I know, on that great getting up morning!"*

John was amazed by the specter's dialect. The fact they each spoke in the reflected period of the 21st century was astonishing to him.

"Excuse me ladies but how is it you and your sister speak in the same manner we do? Correct me if I'm wrong, but, I thought all of you spoke with all the 'thee's and the thou's."

"Psst, John… John," Etta Mae said, casually slapping the man's arm. "You're sadly mistaken, because the Bible was translated from Hebrew and Greek by King James so she never spoke the thee or thee or the thou…"

"So… we're lucky they're even speaking English now!" Donnie added. "Go on Mary finish your story, please."

The biblical icon did a quick curtsey.

"*Thank you, sir.*"

She launched once again into recounting her life's story.

Well… then Jesus said to us; "Take me to where he is laid."

So, then Martha said; "Now surely Lord, my brother smells by now! It's been four days! Then He asked her if she believed on Him, and then she said, "Yes, Lord, I believe."

And off we went.

"You see! I told you guys. Josh exclaimed with enthusiasm. "I was right!"

His remark was met with a loud shush from Etta Mae and Donnie. John was standing with his hand under his chin. He was too perplexed by it all to utter a sound.

"The first thing Jesus did was call to His heavenly Father, whom He always glorified!

I mean the man never made a move without looking to His Father!

"Now that right there is a prime example of how we should be."

Etta Mae said with everyone in agreement.

"Well, then you see, Jesus already knew my brother slept. He even told this to his disciples who couldn't for the life of them, comprehend just what He was saying. They thought He was saying my brother was merely resting in his bed. So, Jesus broke it down. He said to them, "The man is dead, but in order that my Father may be glorified, I will awaken him."

So, when they got there, not only was he dead, but had been for four days. Jesus ordered the stone to be taken away, and after praying, He called; "Lazarus!" Now, I'm glad He called my brother by name; otherwise all the dead would've come forth. Do you feel me?"

"Get a load of this slang; "do you feel me?" You can well bet we feel you." John responded. "And I bet you could hear a pin drop, waiting to see what was coming next. Am I right?"

"John!" Etta Mae shouted. "You're certainly taken a lot of liberty with her."

"Yea, it's not like we're in a scene of the Walking Dead." Josh laughingly said.

"Josh, I'm sure you didn't mean that as a pun." Donnie said, slapping his neighbor a hi-five.

Martha was unable to contain her anxiety suddenly chimed in.

"And then my brother came out of that tomb hopping like this."

The amusing specter did an animated version of a hopping rabbit.

"And my brother was still wrapped in grave clothes mind you, but Jesus even had power over those clothes and ordered them to "lose him!"

Etta Mae's foot instinctively recoiling from the next anticipated jump finished the woman's sentence.

And those grave clothes fell away and glory be to God, your brother was free!"

The out-of-the way remark brought a look of shock to the sisters' faces, prompting Mary to gain control once again.

"*MARTHA!*"

Mary yelled, tearing her eyes from Etta Mae's.

"Let me finish the story... please. Besides, it seems as if we're just confirming what is already known!"

Martha stepping aside allowed her sister to take the lead had one last thing to say.

"She's right though sister. He did. You saw him!"

"Yes, sissy, I did see my brother come out of his tomb... I was there. Remember?"

Mary said pointedly to Martha before addressing the group once again.

"Now... as I was saying; after seeing something like that, who couldn't help but believe Jesus is the Son of God? But, believe you me, just like today, you do have your skeptics."

Etta Mae shaking her head in agreement looked to the men for their reaction, and was obliged with the same gestures.

"Then, after that," Mary continued. *"Jesus had dinner with us again! Could you believe that sissy?*

A shirk of her shoulders was Martha's only response so Mary continued on.

"Our brother Lazarus was there sitting at the head of the table, and sissy here, was busy, as usual. And once again I was at my Lord's feet."

"Yep, there she was."

Martha said, pointing toward the ground.

"Good ole Mary, sitting at Jesus' feet.

She was rewarded with a stern look from her sister.

"Oops! Sorry sis."

Martha nervously shifting from side to side imaginarily zipped her lips.

"Only this time, I was anointing His feet with some costly oil—

"Costly! You want to talk about cost—ly. Ummph!"

"Martha!" Mary shouted. *"Go sit on that rock over there!"*

All eyes followed the direction the stern finger was pointing.

"Oh, darn!"

Sulking, Martha ruefully walked over to the large landscaped rock situated in the center of the lawn and reluctantly sat down.

However, she couldn't help but take notice of the natural feel of the lawn and the neatness of cut flagstones surrounding it.

But, she surmised, there's something different about this stone. The edges were too smooth unlike the many rocks she had climbed upon before.

The proud landscaper sensing her confusion voluntarily offered up an explanation.

"It's not real! It's not a real stone. That rock you're sitting on is a high density Polyethylene Sandstone. You're probably confused because it looks just like the rock your brother's tomb was hewn out of"

As the confused look increased even more on the phantom's face, the proud self taught horticulturist thought it best to further explain.

"What I mean is the rock is manmade. A man made it; we can do that nowadays you know. I can even pick it up."

No one else in the group said a word. Martha simply shrugged her tired shoulders. She sat feeling alone and confused.

The phantom woman's supposed heartache hadn't gone unnoticed by John. Finally, he spoke up.

"Oh, Mary, don't be so hard on your sister. She's just excited. And Donnie, no one gives a damn about your imitation rock."

Donnie's head lowered. Remorsefully he began kicking at the loose sod under his feet. In the grand scheme of things he had all but forgotten about his mole problem.

"Oh, she'll be okay. Besides, she'll soon be over here again being her normal talkative self."

Mary looking long and lovingly over at her lovely sister noticed for the first time, the fine worry lines creasing her sister's delicate forehead. She thought of how well deserved even this short respite would be for her beloved sister

Always a fidgety and a nervous busy body Martha never was prone for sitting at a long length of time. Mary recalled how—

"You were drying Jesus' feet and…"

Etta Mae gesturing with her hands interrupted the apparition's thoughts in hopes of speeding things along.

"Oh, yes!" Mary said taking the hint. *"So I dried His feet with my crown and glory; my hair."*

"Oh! I'm scared of you...who does that; dry a person's feet with their hair? My wife's hair is long, but I bet you won't see her—

The wide-eyed look Josh received from his perturbed female neighbor cut his senseless banter short.

"Oops! Sorry. My bad."

Mary directed her next remark directly to Josh.

"Don't you get it? I didn't do it to show off my long burnish blonde tresses. I was preparing my Lord for His burial."

Not to be outdone Josh felt led to speak up once again.

"Hold up! Hold up! So... exactly, how did you know the Lord was going to die?"

"Dude!" Donnie said intervening. "She said she didn't do anything but sit at the man's feet!"

"And all the while she was sitting there," Etta Mae chimed in. "The Lord was sharing everything with this woman. I would even go so far as to say that's why He personally sent for her."

She turned to Mary and humbly inquired.

"Now, am I right? The Lord knew you knew He would raise your brother even if Martha didn't know. But you had to have known. I'm sure He was counting on your steadfast belief in Him, Mary."

The words Etta Mae spoke cut like a dagger in the phantom's soul. She dropped her head and wept.

The animated exchange was anxiously being observed by the ostracized Martha. On impulse she jumped up and ran to aid her sister.

"How was my sister supposed to know. Even the twelve men that walked, that talked and did everything with the man every day didn't even know?"

"I-I was merely trying to make myself understand, 'tis all—

But the 'Bible-thumper's' try at explaining her statement did little to staunch the flood gates she had inadvertently reopened.

"And I'll tell you something else! After my sister breaks open her 'alabaster box' that contained spikenard, old Judas wanted to know why she didn't sell that expensive oil and give that money to the poor!"

Now recovered, Mary shot her big sister a warning glance, which did little to curtail Martha's restored vigor.

"Like, he was all concerned about 'the poor.' Man! Please!"

Martha's berating of Judas continued on.

"He only wanted to pocket that money to keep for himself! The old thief!"

"Sister!"

"You're kidding, right?" Josh asked unbelievingly. "You mean—

The defiant Martha chose to answer the non-believer's question despite Mary's objection.

Chose to answer it instead.

"But... yes, J-osh, I believe your name is... my sister is right. It's sad to say, but one of Jesus' disciples truly was really a thief. And it just so happened to be... Judas, the group's treasurer."

"Who're you telling?" Etta Mae took the liberty to add. "And all those coins he'd stolen did him little good in the end."

"And Jesus knew along what the man had been doing!"

Martha added, recapturing control of the storytelling.

"Only Judas was the one that didn't know. The old thief!"

"Now be nice Martha."

The whole scenario was still puzzling to the novice newcomer's faith. So Josh asked another question.

"The question I want to know is; why did Jesus give the man the money bag in the first place knowing he was already a thief?"

Martha stumped by the human's question was for once at a loss for words. She gestured for Mary to answer the question.

"Uh, you got this one sis?"

"Well...I'll try." Mary began slowly.

"It was no surprise to Jesus or to the other disciples for that matter their brother was slight of hands. However, if I'm not mistaken, it could've been the fact, Judas' character was being tested, and because Jesus only exhibited truth and honesty before His disciples, it was thought perhaps, Judas would repent and perhaps change his ways.

Martha was so in awe of her sister's wisdom she could only stand listening in silence.

"And if you think about it," Mary continued. *"When you're honest there's no need for you to be tested, because you know you won't steal, nor if you're a truthful person you won't need to be tested, because you know you will not lie."*

The entire group was mesmerized by the iconic Bible figure's thought provoking reply.

It really hit home with Josh and he spoke again.

"Now I get what you're saying… it's like you don't have to test a faithful spouse, because you already know a faithful spouse won't ever cheat! A faithful spouse will always be faithful."

Even though knowing he had been forgiven by God and by Tonika, the once unfaithful husband couldn't help but feel a pang of remorse over the infidelity he had committed.

"Oh, man!" Donnie exclaimed. "You said some deep sh— "Uh hmm. And you're still okay by me dude." He looked to Etta Mae.

"Even I didn't think of it that way. Did you honey?"

"Wha… why no-no, I didn't."

Etta Mae was able to say shaking her head despite being in deep thought. Donnie looked with concern at his wife. He knew her mind was already far ahead of their current discussion.

"You do know honey we all "fall short of His glory" from time to time ourselves."

All involved shook their heads in agreement which prompted Etta Mae to proceed with a question.

"I wonder what would happen if we, you know… if we would all ask the Lord to search our hearts like King David did in Psalm 139?"

Donnie's eye roll did little to end his wife's profound utterance. Donnie's indifference feigned or not to her statement was all but ignored. Etta Mae responded with a pointed look in her husband's direction.

"King David asked God to try him and know his thoughts… Donnie Leroy Smith!"

"Why you look at me? I'm just standing here minding my own business."

"I saw you roll your eyes."

John had been quiet for some time now, but was even mulling the question over in his own mind.

"True, true, you're so right, my sister. And when we do and God reveals the hidden iniquities we never knew we had, it is up us to repent right then and there."

"Amen brother!" Martha responded. *"So, you see my friends, just like we learned."* She said pointedly to her sister, then to the neighbors.

"Even in your time, if you would but call on the name of Jesus, sit at His feet, and get you some of that 'principle wisdom!' Whew! Nothing would be able to stop you!"

The time traveler danced in place as if she was hearing the drowning beat of a church piano or organ reverberating in her head. She stopped long enough to continue her soulful proclamation.

"I'm a witness… ummmph, ummmph, ummmph! Tthat whatever your mountain or your tomb is in life, you just speak to it, and that mountain has to move or that tomb has to give up its hold!" Hallelujah!

A round of applause erupted from all involved.

"Amen and amen! Now that's scripture right there!" Etta Mae shouted.

Encouraged by the mortals' enthusiastic response, Martha even took a bow.

"Thank you, thank you. And whatever you ask of Him, He will do it. But, it will be on His time, because He knows what's best!

But just remember; "He may not come when you want Him. But! When He does come, He'll be right on time!

"Go head girl! Preach!" Now Etta Mae was caught in her spirit induced dance. It all added fuel to Martha's fire.

Oh! How do I know? I'll tell you how. He did it for me, and I know He'll do it for you, because He's an on time God, that's how! Hallelujah!"

The four humans couldn't help but be influenced by the phantom's spirit filled witnessing. A fit of praising and magnifying the Lord broke out right there on the Smith's front lawn.

"Praise Him!" Josh shouted.

"Ain't He alright? Donnie shouted.

"Won He do it?" John shouted.

"Glo-ry! Glory; Glo-ray!" Etta Mae shouted.

To any onlookers passing by or observing from their own windows it looked as if the four humans were in the throes of conniption fits. But little did that matter to the spirit filled praisers. Just like in Luke 10:19 if "Jesus rejoiced in the Spirit" then so could they.

Having made their proclamation, the two sisters left the same way they came; leaving the group in awe. They too go off praising and giving God the glory.

Etta Mae began loudly singing with closed eyes and clapping hands.
"He's an on time God, yes He is.
Oh, oh, oh! He's an on time God;
Yes He i-iz-z!
He may not come when you want Him, but He'll be there right on time.
He'z an on time God; yes He is."

"Honey, honey." Donnie finally said, taking hold of his wife's hands. "We already know He is; trust me... we know. Dottie Peoples already told us."

His companions simply shook their heads respectively and smiled. Feigning hurt, Etta Mae snatched her hand out of her interruptive husband's grip.

"Okay, okay!"

The two stole a quick kiss and embraced.

"Now, you have to admit that was some mountain moving faith right there!" Said Etta Mae.

They all agreed.

"People look at you like you'd 'lost ya' ever loving mind' when you take a praise break like that in our day and time."

"Oh, I don't know about that." John added. "I'm here to tell you; I praise him in the middle of whatever I'm going through, because I know my God can do anything but fail. Just like Martha and Mary we just have to believe!"

His devout proclamation earned him a high five from the seasoned 'Bible-thumper.'

"Look out now John-boy. You stole my line! Mercy!"

John took the liberty to add even more material to the spirit charged atmosphere.

"Well, I have been hearing about people dying, then maybe an hour or two later, come back to life saying they saw a deceased loved one!"

"I bet that's how some people are thinking about that story of the little boy who went to heaven and saw his grandfather."

John covered his mouth to hide a grin.

"It does happen. Shucks! In these days and times anything can happen. Look what we've just gone through."

"You're not kidding. From here on out nothing is going to surprise me."

About that time, John's wife pulling into his driveway honked and waved at the four amigos. MacKenzie was in the back seat. She quickly scrambled to exit the vehicle and ran toward her father.

"Dad-dy!"

"Well, guys that's my cue."

As he turned to leave, Mac jumped into his arms almost causing the equally excited father to lose his balance.

"Whoa! Hey there, munchkin!"

He greeted his baby girl with a big hug and swung her around before planting a big kiss on her cheek.

"Daddy, I missed you!"

Mac whined and grasped her father around the waist.

"Well, I've missed you too munchkin—you have a good time at practice?"

"We-ll…"

Then suddenly her attention span became centered on her next door neighbor.

"Hey, Mr. Donnie, Miss Gretchen's cat is gone.

Donnie couldn't contain his joy after hearing the unexpected news.

"He is!" Then thinking better of his reaction he said more calmly. "Uh hum… I mean; he is? I'm sorry to hear that, Mac."

"Are you re-al-ly Mr. Donnie?"

John chuckled at his daughter's innocent skepticism. Even though her perception of the adult's true nature was on point he took her by the hand before addressing the conversation.

"Yeah, neighbor; I heard about you and Ms. Gretchen's cat!" The amused neighbor said chuckling once more. "I can't believe you were going to kill the little kitty."

"Well… I truly wasn't really going—

Etta Mae, sensing the need to intervene asked Mac about her dance class.

"Max, how was ballet lessons today?"

"Oh, it was good Miss Etta Mae. Only I'm really just begin—"

"Oh, no! Dad, I think I forgot my Pointe shoes!"

The rambunctious youngster suddenly took off running.

"Mom-my!"

"Okay guys, now I really do have to go. Catch you later!"

John ran to catch up with his little sprinter.

"See you later buddy." Donnie said waving good-bye.

"I'm going too."

Josh began backing away to cross the street to his home.

"Tonika and Ashad should be home from shopping soon. That kid is growing like a weed."

He addressed the remaining two, Donnie and Etta Mae before departing.

"But I'm seriously telling you two. We really should get together and figure out all these crazy shenanigans." I've never seen anything like it!"

"You're right Josh. We really should. We've certainly have had some doozies! Have your wife call me so we can plan on where we go from here."

"Alright Etta Mae; I'll certainly have her do that. But knowing my wife she'll be over as soon as she gets home."

They all laughed fully knowing there was truth in his statement.

"Bye Josh."

He waved as he crossed the street. The remaining couple turned to go inside. As they approached the steps Donnie chose that moment to engage his wife in a little jest.

"Honey, I think it's you."

"You think it's me what?"

"I think you must be what's attracting all this paranormal activity around us. It's almost like you're a magnet; like you're a medium or something."

Not the least bit amused, Donnie's remark stopped the Bible-thumper dead in her tracks.

"What!" Etta Mae said whirling around. "Why does it always have to be me? Why do I have to be the medium?"

With a now remorseful spouse in tow the agitated wife wasn't yet finished defending herself.

"And if I'm not mistaken; you, Tonika, Delilah, Damien, and even Josh; all of you've had your own weird contacts. So what does that make each of you?"

"Okay, I'm sorry honey… you're right. I shouldn't have said that. Besides, I didn't mean anything by it. And by the looks of it, if it was true, I wouldn't necessarily call you a 'happy medium' right about now."

Hoping to diminish the amount of damage he'd done with his callous remark the now apologetic spouse decided it best to include himself.

"Heck! You're right. From the looks of it, you'd think we are all mediums. I don't believe either of us are too happy about it though, but still…"

Donnie cradled his wife's head between his hands and smacks her on the forehead. He was so ready to put it all to rest.

Etta Mae returned the loving gesture by wrapping both arms tightly around her husband's waist and squeezed tightly.

"Well… you know honey, if nothing else; it looks like we've at least found that happy medium.

"We have?"

"Yes, dummy, we have. The realm between the supernatural and the natural worlds have been breached. And all of us were fortunate enough to have been a part of it.

"Oh, I don't know about us being fortunate, but yet, it was quite interesting to say the least.

"Look at it this way Donnie. Now we know the hereafter does exist."

"Whew!. I can testify to that. I can truly say to anyone from this day forward; "IT'S SUPERNATURAL!"

Donnie opened the front door allowed his wife to proceed before him.
"It'zzz superna-tural."

Etta Mae whimsically said stepping into the room. Their amusing antics were interrupted by the ringing of Donnie's phone. He answered it on the second ring. Etta Mae looked on inquiringly as to who it could be.

"Hello."

Evidently it was someone he had been wanting to hear from as Donnie broke into a broad smile.

"Hi, ba-bee! It's Janet."

Donnie mouthed to his wife's inquisitive look. She stood listening.

"How're you and Geoffrey doing; work going okay?"

"Good, good to hear. Oh, yes, your mother's right here. You want to speak to her?"

Etta Mae eagerly reached for the phone, but Donnie's hand instinctively went up to block her reach as he was still involved with listening.

"What's that honey? Put you on speaker phone… Okay, here goes."

"Hi Ba-bee." Etta Mae excitedly shouted.

Janet's voice filled the room loud and clear.

"Hi mommy! I miss you. I love you!"

"We miss and we love you too baby." How's Geoffrey?"

"Oh, he's fine… considering…"

Unbeknownst to the delighted parents their son-in-law was also present during the call. Geoffrey yelled out a hearty greeting.

"Hi mom! Hi dad!"

"Hello son!"

They both said simultaneously. But the doting mother-in-law went a tad further.

"It's good to hear your voices. I swear you and my baby stay so busy, I nev—"

"That's just being a doctor mom." But what we were calling about was—

A sense of foreboding gripped the in-laws enough to replace the jubilation of hearing their daughter's distant voice. The waiting couple tensed in anticipation of the outcome.

"Considering what honey; I pray there's nothing wrong. Is there?"

"No mom-my! Silly goose."

They could hear giggling through the phone that appeared to go on forever until Janet finally said.

"No nothing's wrong mom; in fact everything is just right!"

The excitement in their only daughter's voice quickly began to relax tensed nerves.

"But a-are you two sitting down?"

The two quickly found their respective seating.

"Yes, we're sitting down now honey."

"Well...then here goes..."

The air was thick with suspense as moments ticked by. Donnie and Etta Mae was hoping above all hope they were about to hear the words they'd longed to hear it seemed for an eternity.

Then those beautiful words finally came.   *"We-are-preg-nannt!!"*

www.ingramcontent.com/pod-product-compliance
Lightning Source LLC
LaVergne TN
LVHW041852070526
838199LV00045BB/1565